Acclaim for **Donald Antrim**'s

The **Verificationist**

"Donald Antrim is in top form with this high-spirited hallucination, whose characters, undeniably ourselves, carry on engagingly and shamelessly, in an off-the-wall, not to mention off-the-ceiling, environment that is also the world we know, and sometimes wish we didn't."
—Thomas Pynchon

"Wild, silly, funny, confusing, fantastic, challenging. . . . Donald Antrim is a clever and polished writer, and he brings his readers along his strange trajectories with ease and élan." —*Raleigh News & Observer*

"Antrim is the Buster Keaton of current American literature." —*The Wall Street Journal*

"Not since the late Donald Barthelme have we had such a pitch-perfect surrealizing of domestic American life."
—*Esquire*

"[Antrim] weds highbrow rumination and goofy humor, cinematic extravagance and magical realism."
—*The Denver Post*

Donald Antrim

The **Verificationist**

Donald Antrim is the author of two
previous novels, *The Hundred Brothers*
and *Elect Mr. Robinson for a Better World.*
He lives in Brooklyn, New York.

Also by **Donald Antrim**

Elect Mr. Robinson for a Better World
The Hundred Brothers

The **Verificationist**

The Verificationist

A NOVEL

Donald Antrim

VINTAGE CONTEMPORARIES

Vintage Books

A Division of Random House, Inc., New York

FIRST VINTAGE CONTEMPORARIES EDITION, MARCH 2001

The Library of Congress cataloged the Knopf edition as follows:
Antrim, Donald.
The verificationist / by Donald Antrim.—1st ed.
p. cm.
I. Title.
PS3551.N85V4 2000
813'.54—dc21 99-31383
CIP

Vintage ISBN: 0-679-76943-9

Author photograph © Ulrike Schmoni for The New Yorker

www.vintagebooks.com

Printed in the United States of America
10 9 8 7 6 5 4 3 2 1

The **Verificationist**

THE PANCAKE SUPPERS WERE MY IDEA. The plan was, as I imagined it, innocent enough: respectful, unceremonious gatherings, one in early spring a few days before Easter, another sometime after the Wicker Beaver Festival in late October, all the teaching analysts coming together as friends, drinking limitless coffee refills, sharing opinions and impressions of the various candidates at the Institute, of crises or patients' breakthroughs in our private practices, of new ideas relating to the seemingly everlasting task of reconciling classical metapsychology to our particular branch of Self / Other Friction Theory. It was my view that the mood at these pancake affairs should be kept light, and I therefore selected, instead of that new, expensive breakfast restaurant on Woodrow Avenue—Jane had been raving about the food, but I had never set foot inside, for reasons that may be immaterial within the context of the present discussion—the more modest, open-all-night Pancake House & Bar on Eureka Drive, way out past the book factory, down the perilously steep hill leading to our famous covered bridge and, beyond the bridge, the overgrown, abandoned airfield.

It is true that this meant a long drive for my colleagues who live on the north side. An occasional trip through the city's neglected districts is worth their time and trouble. The Krakower Institute, like any privileged organization, has significant responsibilities toward the community, and I can't help feeling that, despite our peer counseling program for teenaged girls, we do not accomplish enough. That said, allow me to report that our first-ever analysts' pancake party was a monumental success. The sordid, oddly lovely, threateningly intimate and utterly unexpected, mortifying embrace between Richard Bernhardt and yours truly did not spoil the evening in the least. Not appreciably, anyway. Everything depends on how you look at these things. I remember that I ordered blueberry pancakes with Canadian bacon, a large orange juice, and, because this was dinner, a house salad. It was, I recall, a gorgeous evening, one of those ideal early-April nights, the stars already apparent in a sky falling from blue to black, the night air brisk with smells of trash fires smoldering in backyard incinerators. You could hear songbirds gathered in the flowering trees that border the restaurant parking lot, and, in the distance, the high, whining buzz made by handmade wood-and-paper airplanes that circled above their pilots, local hobbyists standing on the old airport's broken tarmac, clutching radio consoles.

I love our medium-size city with its Revolutionary War history and its easygoing ways, its minor-league sports teams and its modest skyline—visible now in the distance from my comfortable booth at the Pancake House. Looking north through partly curtained windows, I could see the pyramidal tower of the new municipal hospital, shining brightly, blindingly orange in the setting sun's remaining light.

Beyond the hospital, College Hill rose steeply from downtown and our popular riverfront market district. Lights were on inside homes dotting the Hill's expansive, rolling lawns, which had been hacked out of the region's last native forest back in the early nineteenth century. Kernberg College began, interestingly, as a music academy for orphans; and it is the old music hall, housed in its bizarre, turreted, allegedly haunted mansion atop College Hill, that best captures the benevolent spirit—at least this seemed true to me, that night, looking out at everything from the Pancake House—of our brilliant, glowing city.

"Leave it to you to choose this place for dinner, Thomas."

The speaker was Manuel Escobar, the renowned Kleinian. He sat across from me in the booth by the window, and I explained to him, "Breakfast foods, except for cereals that contain inordinate amounts of sugar, have, in my experience, a comforting, antidepressant quality."

"I suppose that is true if you are an American," said Escobar, looking around the room, then waving impatiently to our beautiful waitress.

"Don't stare."

"I'm not staring, Thomas. I find adolescent girls enchanting, though not compelling. I am happy with Conchita." Then the waitress was beside our table, and Escobar, his eyelids lowered, said, "Hello, I am Escobar, and this is my friend Thomas."

"Pleased to meet you, welcome to the Pancake House & Bar, I'll be your waitress."

"It's nice to be here," I said. Why was I talking? My voice was all wrong, and I felt ridiculous.

Manuel, however—as always so absurdly comfortable with himself, so shamelessly direct in manner—asked, in his coarse, Mediterranean voice, "Tell me, what may we call you?"

"How about Rebecca?"

"Rebecca. May I call you Rebecca? A beautiful name. I would love a cup of your very hot, very strong coffee, Rebecca."

"Cream and sugar with your coffee?"

"Black."

"One black coffee coming up. Anything for you, Thomas?" she asked. She was looking right at me. I fell momentarily in love.

"What? Not yet! Water is fine!"

She wrote in her pad. She handed us menus. She said, "One coffee and one water." She walked off.

"Incredible," I whispered to Manuel after our waitress had marched away on her long legs. Escobar nodded, and I realized he thought I was referring not to him, to his brazen style, but to the girl, her dark good looks. I let the matter drop, since he was, in a way, correct.

"How is your Jane?" he asked me.

Why was I unable to respond with a simple, perfunctory answer to this meaningless, polite question? It was because I was intuitively aware that Escobar wanted to make love to my wife, and I was therefore reluctant to allow him access to her, even through me—especially through me.

Actually, I don't dislike Escobar. It has occurred to me from time to time that an affair between this man and my wife could be harmless enough, and might solve a variety of problems in my home life. I said to him, strategically, "Jane is fond of you. The other night she remarked on how much she likes talking to you. Give her a call, Manuel. Drop by the house."

"No, Thomas. I would not feel in the right place." Escobar sounded sincere, and in spite of the fact that I found his formulation of discomfort alarming (what, precisely, might be "the right place"?—an hourly-rate motel on the highway?), I experienced a brief moment of liking the man intensely; and then the restaurant's front door opened and in came a group of analysts, including Maria, who clacked hurriedly over on her high heels, past the cash register and the little bar area with bottled beers displayed, around the fish tank and the glass case stocked with candies, syrup, and fruit preserves for sale. Around the tables she came. Maria clattered over to our booth, leaned down over the place settings, kissed Escobar on the lips, and announced, "Your paper on sibling murder fantasies among children of recovered alcoholics is extraordinary, Manuel."

"Ah," answered Escobar.

I, for one, am always made uneasy by these rituals of professional approval. I believe established colleagues do well to assume one another's integrity and accomplishment, and leave it at that. I make it a rule never to give people favorable opinions of their work—not even those exceptional, open-minded people who admire my theories concerning reality and its dissolution through polite social conversation.

"He's a genius," said Maria to me. She took off her coat and hung it from a peg near the booth.

"Who's a genius? *Tom?* The Dead Lieutenant?" cried a man standing behind Maria. It was Bernhardt in his red sports jacket and the ridiculous panama hat he never, as far as I can tell, takes off in public. Bernhardt wedged himself into the booth, beside me, and Maria squeezed in next to Escobar, and we all sat quietly—groups that contain Bernhardt, I have found, immediately become anxious, wary, ill at ease; and this is a problem for the man, since he specializes in Group—until Rebecca arrived with Escobar's espresso-strength coffee. I found myself unable not to gaze at this girl's black hair. Was it dyed or natural? I made a mental note to give Rebecca my recruitment speech—sometime later, in private, without all these shrinks around to make her feel inadequate or insecure—for my Young Women of Strength program at the Krakower Institute.

In the meantime, to irritate Bernhardt—and to get him back for using an old nickname that I'd rather not hear—I said, "I agree with Maria. Manuel is one of our important thinkers."

After that I felt depressed, as I knew I would after praising an associate, or even an intimate.

In fact, Escobar is a shrewd, insightful, compassionate therapist. One might wish he would become less involved in patients' lives outside the consulting room (the recent, unsettling incident with Mrs. Jackson and the countersigned insurance claim checks comes to mind); however, Escobar is a European. His unorthodox, interdisciplinary methods naturally reflect some sort of traditional cultural orientation.

"You're that party of doctors from the mental institute, aren't you?" Rebecca said.

"That's right," answered Bernhardt, giving me a wonderful chance to contradict him on a fine point. I knew I shouldn't've—you have to watch your step with Bernhardt; he's grandiose and will lose his temper and, on occasion, shout—but it was irresistible.

"We're not doctors. At least, I don't think anyone at our table has a medical degree," I said, looking around at the faces of my companions.

Bernhardt said, "Tom, I don't know about you, but I have a Ph.D. in clinical psychology." Food had not yet been served, and already Richard was getting worked up over genital potency issues.

I explained to our waitress, "It's true that we are clinical psychologists. Those with doctorates may call themselves doctors if they choose, but most of us, except Sherwin of course, are not doctors in the way that people routinely think of doctors."

She—bless her heart—recalled, "I had this jerk for a history teacher in eleventh grade. He got a Ph.D. through the mail or somewhere and then made everyone call him *Doctor* Woody."

"My Ph.D. is *not* mail-order." Bernhardt's face beneath his panama hat was suddenly, brilliantly red.

"Richard, it's all right. Take it easy." Maria reached across the tabletop and stroked Bernhardt's sleeve, lightly, reassuringly, professionally.

"How can I take it easy? Tom has no idea how to get along with peers. I worked hard for my Ph.D. It gets so I'm afraid to take pride in my accomplishments."

"Tom didn't mean to hurt your feelings, Richard. I'm certain he respects your credentials. Isn't that right, Tom?" asked Maria, the diplomat.

"Sure."

At that point, more analysts barged in. Peter Konwicki, Elizabeth Cole, Dan Graham, Terry Kropp, Mike Breuer—and Dr. Sherwin Lang, the gynecologist turned psychiatrist, whose relationship with alcohol may or may not have been getting in the way of his relationships with analysands. Greetings were transacted, and the Bernhardt situation was momentarily defused as, one after another, adjacent tables filled with personnel. Someone put money in a tableside jukebox and a popular tune played. The waitresses in their blue dresses came and went, shouldering dinner plates and metal trays stacked with silverware. Our waitress approached and said, "Ready, Doctors?"

"Two eggs over easy with hash browns and extra cinnamon-raisin toast with butter on the side," said Bernhardt.

"The country sausage and eggs, I guess," Maria said next.

"How do you want your eggs?"

"Scrambled. Please."

Manuel requested more coffee, nothing but black coffee, and then it was my turn.

"Well, I'm torn between the blueberry pancakes and the eggs Benedict. Are the blueberries fresh?"

"Yes, sir."

"Treat yourself to pancakes, Lieutenant," said Bernhardt.

I explained, "I like pancakes, but with pancakes a little goes a long way. They leave me feeling stuffed."

"I know what you mean."

"On the other hand, whenever I have the chance to order them, and I don't, I regret it."

Rebecca waited. My Institute associates glared at me, and the noisy room got, I thought, quieter. I was in danger of acute vacillation and could feel my face growing hot, the skin tingling. Choice, with its inevitable invitations to loss, is always such a trial. It does not matter, in my experience, that a particular choice consists in apparently unweighty alternatives. Quite the opposite. Choices between banalities are some of our more intimidating ordeals in life. We all know how the simplest dilemmas can lead, through symbolic and emotional pathways in the unconscious, to larger, often painful issues facing us at work and at home. Let's take an example, a hypothetical case, from home. Or, better yet, let's not. A discussion of theory can only be weakened by intimate, possibly humiliating revelations. The simple example I was going to give— involving an unpainted room and a drawer full of paint chips in assorted pastels and flat whites—is not only *not simple,* it is loaded to capacity with marital sorrows and the profoundest mysteries of destiny, accident, and the overall purpose and meaning of life. Here's what I mean. I will attempt to remain objective. An upstairs room needs painting. The room is quite cozy, with attractive floors and a view of trees and neighboring yards. But its walls, blemished with scuffs, spackle, and dirt, have been an eyesore for a long, long time—ever since the present owners (Jane and I, naturally) first occupied this little house (17 Granite Farm Road, second on the left after the empty, boarded-up community center swimming facility, where neighborhood teenagers go to have sex and smoke dope), this little house with its blazing-red front door and "stovepipe" mailbox and the handsome attic dormers that remind you, as you climb the drive bordered by stone fences left from times when these hills were farm country, of ships' portholes. It will take an afternoon, two at most, to prep and paint the room behind the pretty windows. Painted, the room might be comfortably used as a small, sunlit study. Nevertheless, years have passed and the room remains vacant, destitute, unclean; its door is rarely opened. Downstairs, in the kitchen, beneath knives in a drawer, lies a manila envelope holding paint chips. Colors range from the cool whites and baby blues to lemon yellows and delicate salmons. The wife in question (Jane) insists any color is fine with her. Her (Jane's) husband (I) secretly suspect(s) this is not the case. He (I) think(s) she (Jane) wants a sturdy, masculine blue, because he (I) feel(s) that she (Jane) is secretly hoping for a baby (ours) to live in this room, and he (I) suspect(s), judging from other things known about her (the wife)—things better not explored in depth at this moment—that she (my beloved) would, without a doubt, favor a boy. I (a boy myself, once; currently a grown man who, like all men, experiences many conflicts, doubts, and insecurities in life) have (has) the usual, probably stereotypical fears and reservations about infant children and boys in particular—the added financial strain; the inevitable displacement of the man (me again!) by another (my own baby boy, no less), leading to diminished sexual relations, growing jealousy, fits of general desperation, and eventual panic, leading (if I know myself at all) to flight (most likely to one of the chain motels along the highway leading west from town) as a form of retaliation, followed in due course by return, contrition, reconciliations, the conscience-stricken attempts at repair, and, finally, resumed couples counseling with Maria—as well as certain distinctly *personal* terrors that derive from my own history as a child coming of age in an environment (home of origin, with all *its* problems) that is currently being reviewed and, to large extent, relived—in my marriage, in my work with patients, in my own ongoing analysis with old Dr. Mandelbaum—an environment in which I (the gloomy, doubting boy I once was) obviously failed to reach the depressive position and subsequently develop a number of the crucial interpersonal insights and skills associated with mature behavior. This is not, as you can see, turning out to be a particularly simple example—the unpainted room as repository of unspoken thoughts, symbolic home and playroom to unborn generations that will supersede and finally bury us when, ancient, decrepit, and delirious, we die—especially when you consider the ways that inner conflicts manifest, in close relationships, as vulnerabilities. Jane reflexively accommodates my fears and desires, as I do hers; together, man and wife, we collude in a mutual conspiracy to shelter and protect one another from our own and each other's inevitable and final abandonment. The simple question "What color do you want to paint that upstairs room?" might, if we follow things to their logical conclusions, be stated: "How do I live, knowing that I will one day die and leave you?"

"I don't know! I don't know!" I shouted at my Pancake House table companions. My breath was short and my hands were chilled; sweat broke out on my arms and my back, and I felt overcome with guilt.

"Easy, Lieutenant," said Bernhardt. He sounded genuinely concerned and also a little frightened. He suggested, "Look, buddy, you can pick from both sides of that menu."

"I can?"

"Yes," said Rebecca.

"Really?"

It was true. Why hadn't I considered this? I asked, "Will it cost extra?"

"There's a two-dollar charge for combination plates." Rebecca had such a sweet manner.

"Two dollars. That's not so *baaad,*" said Maria in a childish voice; she was, as we say in the psychology trade, talking me down.

I took a deep breath. I took another. "Okay. This is a pancake restaurant. Bring me some blueberry pancakes."

Easy as that, it was done, and I felt the awful pressures subside, and I was able, almost miraculously, to make subsequent, smaller choices. Breath by gentle breath, my calm returned. I placed my order as, outside the window, the world turned dark. It was suppertime, and the buzzing of model aircraft had ceased; those wood-and-paper planes had made their final landings on the ancient airport's broken runways. Beyond the runways, city lights sparkled. Birds in the trees cried and sang. Past the trees, in the distance, the hospital glowed in sunlight; it was our lighthouse.

Inside, the lights shone brightly, and noises were getting louder, as my Institute colleagues called out to one another, yelled from table to table across the room. It was terrific to see everyone drinking coffee and laughing, and I felt, as I rarely do anymore, that the mental health community is made up of gracious, affable men and women.

My pleasant mood did not last. I am afraid that I am not inclined toward a merry or carefree outlook. This is not to say that I do not enjoy life. On the contrary, my work gives me pleasure. Every now and then, on fine days when the air is cold and clear and sweet with smells of the first pollen from the blossoming trees, when the late-afternoon sun casts its rays through high purple or white clouds, and lights from office buildings reflect off the winding, icy river, when everything in the world looks magnificently, radiantly silver, as if lit from within—the trees, the cars, the haunted music building on the hill—in that luminous hour before dark, after the long day and before night's descent, then the problems in my marriage do not seem insurmountable, because on those evenings I feel ready for sex.

Sometime soon, if I can find the time, I would like to draft a formal paper proposing air temperature, cloud cover, barometric pressure, moisture levels, wind speed, etc., as authentic relational constructs—the atmospheric versions of "other people," in effect—with roles in ambient mood formation that are exactly analogous to archetypal roles played by human parents, siblings, lovers, sworn enemies, and so on. In my

Climate Relations scenario, a malady like Seasonal Affective Disorder (in which emotional states vary on a calendric schedule, according to weather and light, the length or shortness of days, the yearly anniversaries marking traumatic or other formative experiences) can be more accurately diagnosed—and, I believe, effectively treated—as a special form of interpersonal crisis. This idea will be recognized by professional critics as a militant extension of Object Relations Theory in psychoanalysis. Some colleagues, objecting on grounds of anthropomorphism, will undoubtedly insist that I go too far when I suggest that high humidity acts on our inner life in the same manner as a wrathful mother. Lay readers will, I trust, comprehend, instinctively, the truth in these principles.

"Tom, my friend, I think you ordered the right thing. Those blueberry pancakes look good," said Bernhardt after the food arrived. I did not enjoy the way the man leaned into my territory when he spoke—the dry breath on my cheek, the hat brim almost grazing my head—but, in spite of this, I felt touched by the awkwardness of Bernhardt's transparent goodwill tactics.

"Have a bite."

"I couldn't."

"Go ahead, Richard. There's more here than I can eat. Dig in."

"I've got dried eggs all over my fork, Tom. Why don't you cut me off a section?"

"Richard, take a bite. Please. I don't care about the eggs," I lied, shoving my pancakes toward him down the table, establishing distance under cover of generosity.

"Do you want some of these eggs, Tom?"

"No, thanks."

"Toast?" asked the Group counselor.

"No toast for me."

"Cinnamon-raisin toast. I've got plenty."

"I see. How many slices of toast do you have there, Richard? Seven? Eight?"

"This sausage is good," said Maria, getting into the conversation. "Tom? Sausage?"

"I'll pass, Maria."

"Is that sausage hot?" asked Bernhardt. The man was without shame. He turned toward me and said, "You've got a nice piece of ham here, Lieutenant."

"That's Canadian bacon."

"Is that what it is? It's delicious, isn't it? Not as spicy as Maria's sausage. You can pour syrup on the sausage to tone it down," Bernhardt said, chewing.

Escobar, watching Bernhardt eat from other people's plates, wore the clinician's slightly engaged, slightly weary expression. What did he think, in moments like these, of Americans?

It is worth considering, in light of this question, the ways that national, ethnic, and religious prejudices express, on a larger scale, the tendency among people in relationships to sicken and enrage one another. "What does Escobar think of Americans?"might be interestingly restated: "How can Judy Bernhardt dine with her husband without wanting him dead?"

"Oh, dear. I ate too much meat. I can feel my heart struggling to push the blood through the veins," sighed Bernhardt. And, truly, the big man looked unwell. Moisture beaded his forehead; his small eyes had become enlarged and protrusive; and his breathing was, all of a sudden, rapid, shallow, alarmingly loud.

"Richard? Are you feeling all right?" asked Maria, doubtless concerned that Bernhardt was choking.

This man leaned back from the table; he managed a lengthy, sucking inhalation, a sound horrible to hear. "Better in a minute—catch my breath—piece of your hot sausage—stuck," sputtered Bernhardt. Saliva, a clotted spray, discharged from his mouth. What was the right thing to do? Strike the man on the back? I reached out, raised my hand to wallop Bernhardt's shoulder blades, and Maria exclaimed, "Tom, don't!"

"No?"

Bernhardt's face was the color of blood. His eyes looked ready to fly from their sockets. I was disappointed at not being allowed to hit him.

Maria explained, "Slapping a person on the back can dangerously lodge a foreign particle in the esophagus." I could not help imagining that were Rebecca nearby, she would get a clear demonstration of the fact that we were not, any of us, bona fide doctors, or even competent in an emergency. Only Manuel remained unperturbed. Manuel always carries and expresses himself with great poise. He said to our colleague, "Listen to me. Are you listening? Swallow."

We waited while Bernhardt gulped. The man was under great strain. He wasn't suffocating—not yet.

"Swallow," said Manuel again. "Swallow." Hearing Manuel's voice, I could not help thinking about our waitress, about the way Manuel had ordered coffee from her; and I imagined, then, Manuel's voice speaking in a whisper, seductively, to my Jane:

"I love to look at your back. You are so beautiful. Tom does not appreciate your beauty. He is a fool. Now lean forward and hold tightly to the banister," I imagined Manuel saying to her.

The atmosphere was tense. Complex power dynamics were at work. Bernhardt, by threatening to fatally gag on other people's food, had taken the role of usurper, "capturing" not only the food but the sympathies of his peers. Unfortunately for him, there was not space in the booth for me to wrap my arms around his body, to reach over, if necessary, and squeeze him hard. Bernhardt's stomach pressed against the table's edge. He held cinnamon-raisin toast in one hand and his napkin in the other. He made a noise in his throat, and this noise sounded beautiful, forlorn, like faraway bagpipes or wind in trees. As if in response to Bernhardt's sound, Maria leaned forward across the tabletop; she leaned toward the fat man. She looked as if she might weep. She did not touch Bernhardt; Maria's hands stopped short of touching; they floated, tentative, in the air near Richard's face. What beautiful fingers she had. I felt, looking at Maria's face and those hands, as if I were a trespasser witnessing something wonderful and mysterious.

In this way it became clear—from this tableau made by these two: the man struggling for breath; the woman craning toward him; and their lovely stillness as, for a moment, they regarded one another—it became clear, in the way these things become, in such a public moment, oddly, inexplicably clear to others, that Maria and Bernhardt were sleeping together.

Or was it conceivable that I only imagined this scenario (the scenario and my perception of it), because I had actually perceived—in ways that I did not understand and could not account for, that evening over pancakes, bacon, and a salad—that Manuel, our Kleinian across the table, was already sleeping with my wife?

In other words, had Manuel somehow told me a truth about his involvement with Jane, without telling me anything at all? And was it not possible, even likely, if this was so, that everyone was sleeping with everyone—including Bernhardt and Maria? The question I am raising is this: Did my belief that my Institute colleagues were lovers come from observation and recognition of subtle interpersonal signals, the unconscious communications between them, or did it come from inside *me,* from my own barely perceptible feelings and awarenesses, those feelings that I was not, at the time, fully alert to, feelings about Manuel, about Jane, about sex and rivalry in sex, about the strange and precarious nature of human relationships, about the excruciating complexities of infidelity, stolen ecstasy, and guilt?

"Swallow."

Bernhardt shuddered; his Adam's apple rose, then fell. Food, it seemed, went down. Muscles in Bernhardt's neck relaxed, and he raised his napkin and spit out more food he had not forced down. This food he wrapped, meticulously, in the napkin. The crisis was over and we all leaned back in our seats. Bernhardt took a drink from his water glass and said, "That always happens."

I felt, in that instant, unable to remain in a booth with this overweight father figure. "Richard, would you excuse me for a minute?"

"Sure thing, Lieutenant. You want to get up?" asked Bernhardt before biting toast—the man still eating in spite of the problems eating caused.

"Yes. And, Richard, I'd appreciate it if you wouldn't call me Lieutenant. It reminds me of something I'd rather not think about."

"What's the big deal, Tom? That was years ago. It's not like you killed anybody. Stabbing that guy out at the Grove was an accident."

"That's not the point."

Bernhardt waved his toast in the air, a little motion presumably indicating that he would move aside as soon as he finished chewing. Others in the noisy restaurant raised forks and cups, but my appetite was gone; life felt wretched to me. Maria, a beauty when younger and still handsome in her forties—stylishly dressed, carefully made up and wearing good shoes, that sort of thing—appeared, to my eyes, that night at the Pancake House & Bar, tired and a little displeased, aged somehow: by time, naturally, but also by disappointment; by, I suppose you could say, the disappointments of living. Her mouth as she ate worked slowly. With each new bite, Maria's tongue came out, far out, in the manner of a tongue at the onset of fellatio, one of those intense, illicit blow jobs she used to give whenever the two of us could slip away, late on an afternoon, to the Institute's book and manuscript vault, the subcellar archive with no windows, back in our early days as Institute trainees. Out came the tongue to meet the food on the fork. Maria's tongue was thick and blue, you could say purple almost; and it had the blunted, rounded contours of a medium-size putty knife. Here was a tongue that, believe me, kissing, could really fill your mouth. Now food previously taken in, little spots of wet color, clung to its surface.

And so the erotic in memory becomes, at a later stage in life, unseemly. Again and again Maria's tongue emerged, met, then blanketed and enveloped, the lump of oncoming fried sausage, or the scrambled eggs, or a piece of potato; next it slowly withdrew, a violet thing luring the fork toward Maria's mouth. Fillings were visible, silver, shimmering; and I could see, deep in her mouth, that dead tooth that had gone brown. It is probably true that I would not have been so disturbed by Maria's mouth, her chewing and swallowing, had I not wished, maybe for old times' sake, as they say, to feel, again, that heavy tongue pushing past her teeth, past *my* teeth.

Have you ever noticed?—people, no matter how beautiful or desirable, invariably will, if observed closely while going about their daily business of keeping alive, begin to seem like monsters.

Bernhardt was not moving from the booth. I watched him eat. It would not be wrong to say that I was, in a manifestly physical sense, sickened by the sight.

"Thomas, what are you doing?" asked Escobar.

"I'm afraid I'm not feeling well, Manuel. I think I need to

walk around. I'll be fine if I get some air." I turned my body. I secured a grip on the seat back, then hoisted my feet, first the left, then the right foot, out from beneath the low tabletop. I bent my knees and raised my legs. I rested my shoes on the seat. I was working in a tight space. "Watch out, Richard. Don't move." I half stood on the seat and, leaning sideways against the seat back, keeping my balance, taking care not to knock Bernhardt in the head, wormed one leg, the left, up, over, and down into the vacant booth behind. From there it was an easy slide into the empty seat and freedom. I saw coworkers watching me, and I noticed our waitress watching too, and I waved to her and shrugged my shoulders and rolled my eyes and made a goofy face and a lot of relatively meaningless hand gestures in the air, and she smiled.

Bernhardt took another distressed breath. "Do you see what I mean, Maria? The man has no regard for social protocols. He's like a two-year-old!"

I have to admit that this was, as a diagnosis, pretty much correct. I have found, however, that it is best to understand Bernhardt's criticisms and complaints—no matter how flattering, when considered in the right context—as nothing more than self-administered medications against the man's own terror of vitality, autonomy, playfulness, the life force in any form. I stood and said, "This is a pancake restaurant, Richard."

"What the hell has that got to do with it?"

I spoke to Bernhardt—spoke, as well, to the entire room, all my Krakower Institute peers gathered around tables stacked with dishes and balled napkins and half-empty cups.

Waitresses circled, offering refills. Strangers at distant booths stopped talking, finished chewing, and attended to my improvised discourse.

"What is a pancake? Cooked batter, covered in sugar and butter. Condiments are applied to it. It is food. But it is not as a food, not as sustenance, that we crave the pancake. No, the pancake, or flapjack if you will, is a childish pleasure; smothered in syrup, buried beneath ice cream, the pancake symbolizes our escape from respectability, eating as a form of infantile play. The environments where pancakes are served and consumed are, in this context, special playrooms for a public ravenous for sweetness, that delirious sweetness of long-ago breakfasts made by mother, sweetness of our infancy and our great, lost, toddler's omnipotence. Look around. Notice, if you will, these lighting fixtures suspended from the ceiling like pretty mobiles over a crib. Notice the indestructible plastic orange seating materials designed to repel spills and stains. Notice these menus that unfold like colorful, laminated boards in those games we once played on rainy days at home, those unforgettable indoor days when we felt safe and warm, when we knew ourselves, absolutely, to be loved. We come to the Pancake House because we are hungry. We call out in our hearts to our mothers, and it is the Pancake House that answers. The Pancake House holds us! The Pancake House restores us to beloved infancy! The Pancake House is our mother in this motherless world!"

I reached down and grabbed a handful of cinnamon-raisin toast from Bernhardt's plate. I surveyed the room. It was tempting, very tempting, to fire a round at Sherwin Lang. On the other hand, for reasons having to do with alcoholism—the paranoia and grandiosity, all the thought disorders and the ugly volatility associated with that common disorder—this was a bad idea. Elizabeth Cole looked stunning with her black hair falling around her face, only barely hiding her large, provocative ears. Hitting her with food would be a disturbingly powerful sexual gesture.

"Don't do what I think you're thinking of doing, Tom," warned Bernhardt behind me.

I calculated the distance—three square tables covered with blue cloths and placed corner to corner, a diamond pattern allowing waitress-and-tray-width walking grids between and around each table—to Peter Konwicki's head. The child psychologists all saw what was coming and hid behind menus. I said to Bernhardt, "You've got to relax and have fun for a change, Dick."

"Don't call me Dick."

I felt a hand on my arm. It was Bernhardt's. This man's hand grasped my arm—the fingers wrapping tightly around my forearm, pinching my arm—so that I could not move or shake free to throw the toast.

"Get your hands off me, Richard."

"Drop the bread, Tom."

As always, when dealing with an unpleasant dispute over professional conduct or ideology—ours was, after all, a *professional* pancake gathering—I looked, hopefully, to other factions for support.

"Tom, Richard is right. We don't want a food fight tonight. I'm sure it would be a tension reliever, but everyone is already having such a pleasant evening. Can't we just drink our coffee?" This from Maria, who said to our foreign companion, "More coffee, Manuel?"

Escobar watched me and Bernhardt (watched my arm held so tightly in Bernhardt's hand) the way he watched everything in life—inscrutably, intelligently—and it was impossible not to admire his competence as a speaker in an adopted language when he said, "Thomas embraces a revolutionary spirit in his work. We must not ask him to behave otherwise in society. Let him hurl these pieces of toast like new and radical ideas that must be cast into the world. Pieces of toast like angry children who will hit us and upset us and change our ways of thinking and feeling."

"Thank you, Manuel," I said, tugging my arm, trying to break loose and lob a Hail Mary shot over the open menus barricading the child psychologists. It was all too much for Bernhardt. The man heaved himself up from his seat and, in a rash and impulsive moment, seized me in a bear hug. His arms wrapped around me. It was fantastic to be held by this man with the huge body and the arms that squeezed and squeezed.

My hands were pinned to my sides. Bernhardt's stomach against my back felt soft, warm, repulsive. The man inhaled and grew larger; and it was as if he were ballooning, growing immense with air. I sank into him. I could hear his wheezing as he breathed, the oxygen going in, the blood-heated exhalations streaming out. His hat's brim pressed against my head, and I could smell a perfume of geraniums—or maybe lilies?—in the mixture of Bernhardt's breath, his sweat and his clothing, the shampoo and shaving lotion. He rested his chin against my shoulder, and we swayed from side to side, and I breathed the man's scents while his arms crushed my ribs.

Breathing got difficult, and I said, whispering, "Please, let go."

Looking across the restaurant, I saw friends and strangers, the analysts and the waitresses and, near the door, an intact family with small children, and, also, a young couple—attractive, sullen teenagers killing time in a corner. No one, not even our busy Rebecca, ate or moved or looked away from the humiliating spectacle of Bernhardt lifting me a foot or more off the floor, Bernhardt holding me high in the air, cradling me.

For a moment I hung there. Bernhardt, his breath tickling the hairs sprouting from my ear, whispered:

"Say uncle."

That was when I felt the sadness coming on. It was not surprising, given the circumstances. How often are we, as adults, raised up and carried like babies—in public!—softly spoken to by a man whose face we cannot see, a man who is enormous and powerful, terrifying, as he holds us aloft? Try this sometime if you don't believe me when I say that the experience will make you weep with sorrow and regret for all the trouble you have caused—will cause—the people most dear to you. My thoughts, naturally, went to Jane. Here came Jane, the image of her, filling my mind and my heart, that night in the Pancake House, that evening in Bernhardt's arms—*Jane! Jane!*—filling my heart with pity and shame. She is not a monster to me. Not at all. I am the one, not she, who remains, after all our years together, frightened by love. Or I should say that I am frightened, and so is Jane; we are frightened in our different though complementary ways. Sometimes, on an evening in winter, when the house is only dimly lit by reading lamps and the fire burning in our fireplace, I might happen to see her standing idly in the living room's soft half-glow, her face lit by firelight and her body veiled in shadows that flicker then disappear; or, later, insomniac and anxious in the cold night hours, I might peer down on her as, wrapped in sheets, she sleeps; or, the next day, a rainy, windy day at home, I will hear footsteps on creaking floorboards overhead—Jane upstairs, walking back and forth, doing some small thing, shutting windows against the storm—and during these or a thousand similar household moments, interludes of relative quiet, of no apparent consequence insofar as nothing consequential is taking place, I will be struck, swiftly, deeply, absolutely, with the presence of her—I don't know what else to call this—her bodily presence and the weight in the room, in the house, of another life, her life, charged as it is with her feelings and thoughts, the lonely, playful, idiosyncratic and remarkable moods that seem, as moods (especially bad moods) do, virtually to radiate outward from her—I believe this is what people mean when they talk about a person's spirit—permeating the air and turning the whole environment into an arena of sexuality and heat. I share in this. We are together. Sex presses in. Would a picture of Jane make things more concrete? Her breasts, always beautiful to me, have, I think, grown fuller and more gorgeous over the years; they look as they might if she were pregnant. Lately she leaves her hair unbrushed, a brown-

and-gray snarl that cascades over her eyes and down around her bare white shoulders. Jane has recently taken to backless dresses—she wears them around the house!—and I am tormented, even in the frigid winter months, by the network of large and tiny moles that range from the base of her spine up her lower back, a dark arabesque of shaded blemishes, benign, interconnected birthmarks that combine, in a certain light, to resemble, to my mind, a kind of reduced, miniaturized, monochromatic landscape—a greatly shrunken Bierstadt or a Winslow Homer painting, I sometimes think, one of Homer's grand Atlantic Oceans, night falling over the sea and a mist descending to obscure little fishermen in their boats, men far from home, away from shore, adrift on waves that crash across my wife's lumbar region as she bends down to stroke the cat. I've been staring at Jane's birthmarks for a long time, and it stands to reason that I detect in these forms a coherence and meaning that other people would not appreciate. But I am straying from the scene at hand: Bernhardt, the obese Group counselor, the Ph.D., hugging me to him like a father hugging his baby girl. What strength this man had! His arms—one red coat sleeve crossed over the other—were wrapped around me, encircling me; his hands' open palms pressed against my belly and my ribs. He squeezed and the breath went out of me and I felt dizzy and sick to my stomach. I leaned back, turned my head, and peered over Bernhardt's shoulder; I gazed, from my high perch, helplessly down at our table. I could easily see that unhealthy still life made from sticky plates and empty glasses, saltshakers and butter dishes, our knives and spoons and the paper napkins blotted with coffee and orange marmalade and eggs already fading to brown, the napkins stained with food and, in the case of Maria's spread like a shroud across her plate, stained with lipstick, the scarlet impression of Maria's unsubtle kiss. Bernhardt the horrible father whispered into my ear, "You're nothing but trouble, Tom. That's why we love you. I know it may surprise you to hear that we love you, but it's true. I'll say it again. We're your coworkers, and we love you. Sometimes, though, you get carried away and you have to be stopped, Tom, because when you get carried away, when you go too far and play too hard, then things get out of control, and when things get out of control, everyone feels bad. Why does everyone feel bad? I'll tell you why. When you start climbing across the furniture or throwing toast or spitting water at people, all those silly things you like to do around the office or during important meetings or at dinner parties, then the world gets crazy and unpredictable, and everyone around you, all the people who love you, we all get swept up in your craziness, and before long we feel sad. We feel sad and lost. We know what it means to be you, Tom."

"You do?" I whispered. Breathing was hard, and plates on the table looked nauseating beneath overhead light.

"Yes, Tom. We do," confided Bernhardt, applying another squeeze. I had the sense that Bernhardt was using me, that night, as a fragile, middle-aged totemic object signifying childhood and—if I know him, with his fondness for D. W. Winnicott, the Squiggle game, and various improvisational-play theories that owe a lot to so-called radical avant-garde theater and the whole "process over performance" approach to role playing and creative living in general—Bernhardt was using me, as I was saying, as a human totem signifying childhood and the depression that grows with the healthy child's capacity for love and hatred in mature relationships. I know that Bernhardt employs dolls, sandboxes, crayons, and various stuffed animals in his practice with adults, often with remarkable results. Now I was the doll, Bernhardt the big man holding me; and the world, because I floated above it, became magical and safe.

I was sweating. I felt cared for. My hand opened. The cinnamon-raisin toast, the few slices of toast, dropped, broken and inedible, to the floor.

"That's better," growled the voice in my ear, the menacing, nurturing, comforting voice of the adult.

I placed my hands over Bernhardt's. It is true that my arms were pressed beneath Bernhardt's arms wrapped tightly around me. Nonetheless, my poor arms were free, more or less, from the elbows down; in other words, I was able to move my hands a small distance, to wiggle my trapped arms, and to reach up and hold those hands holding me.

My palms were dusted with crumbs. I wiped the crumbs on Bernhardt. People were watching, the entire crowded, silent restaurant. I understood, gazing sadly at my colleagues' faces, that this was an occasion for embarrassment. But why? For what reason?

I felt woozy. It was as if I were far, far off the floor. I closed my eyes and hyperventilated—a dozen short breaths. I did not ask Bernhardt to set me down. Standing unsupported was, I felt, out of the question; and I had the impression, anyway, that I was drifting upward, rising farther and farther from the ground.

It was then, while Bernhardt squeezed and I held him—it was then that I began my ascent toward the ceiling. Up I went. I have to confess that I felt, ascending, a bit scared. I am not as a rule happy or comfortable on rocking boats or on airplanes thrown by turbulence, or on the average amusement-park ride, or even cruising in an automobile on a hilly lane; and I can say from experience—I think people who endure motion sickness will concur—that the first sensations of nausea are invariably accompanied by a swift and debilitating panic, a flush of hotness and fear that grows intense and then becomes a chief symptom of the illness. It is true—and on this point, as well, I believe fellow sufferers will agree—that the worst motion sickness occurs when one is helpless to predict or control the rising and the falling, the dipping and soaring and that sudden, excruciating ascension of a speeding car or tossing plane, or the awful pitching and rolling on board a rusty boat. The worst sickness comes when one is a passenger.

Bernhardt squeezed and up I went, up toward the Pancake House ceiling, drifting higher to float over the heads of clinicians and waitresses gathered around tables piled with waffles, uneaten bacon, biscuits. How I wished I had been sensible and ordered eggs over easy. But it was too late, the pancakes were inside me, and I was hovering beneath the ceiling, up beneath pendulous, institutional lights, and the air against my face felt warm and still, and friends' faces below me appeared pale and minuscule, and I could smell Bernhardt's soap and his dry skin, those bad clothes and the man's breath like too-sweet flower petals brushing my face, filling my nose and my mouth with rotten perfume. I felt the big man's arms wrapped around me. I held on as best I could, reached up with my hands and clasped his tightly in mine to keep from floating too high or, alternatively, from losing balance and falling forward across chairs and tables. Outside, the wind stormed in off the silver river that flows through our city; and I imagined, briefly and stupidly, that if I could only sail over near a window, I might be carried out of the Pancake House, back toward town and, with any luck, home—up and away over the delightful covered bridge and the book factory and surrounding neighborhoods crowded with porno theaters, tattoo parlors, all those intriguing and dangerous barrooms—straight back to Jane.

Possibly, the wind might carry me away from Jane. Out over Battlefield Grove, for instance, with its gloomy walking trails through dense, uncut forest, and its prominent, hilltop cannon aimed directly, perpetually, toward the prehistoric burial mound in the valley below.

It occurred to me that flying on the wind was a precious, extremely literary idea—not in the least the sort of psychological concept I can feel good about—and that, furthermore, even if it were truly possible to travel through the air, a very short journey of this nature would, undoubtedly, leave me sick as a dog, as they say.

At this point I knew that I had gone into an emotionally disassociated state—exactly the kind of out-of-body condition that is seen among victims of trauma or abuse.

Bernhardt, whether alert to this fact or not, was attempting to destroy me, apparently through some form of metaphoric patriarchal rape. The intimacy between us was real and devastating. I was, I felt, in danger of a psychoneu-rotic splitting off—a costly form of self-protection—the proof of which was my thoroughly tactile appreciation of the man's proximity, of his body's pressure, its aggressive and hot con-tact with mine; and, simultaneous with this recognition of our physical linking, my utterly convincing sensation of incorpo-real ascension and a perceived flight, or something like a flight—a subjective projection of, I suppose, for want of a bet-ter word, the Self—out from my body, away from the hideous man, toward the restaurant's foam-tile ceiling, toward the roof and around the room. I say "the man" rather than "Richard Bernhardt" because I believe that, to a large extent, the threat to my sanity was not *personal* in the usual meaning of that word, but generic and rooted in unconscious life.

I loved this awful man, and he was deeply in love with me. In order to bear this knowledge and the attendant physical violation, our embrace, I had no recourse but escape into a transient psychotic breakdown and its exhilarating symp-toms. Was this, my withdrawal from tenderness, what was meant by "astral projection"? Could I, in this momentary awakening to love, break the bonds of gravitation, soar heavenward, and explore the unknown, infinite Universe?

It was certainly worth a try. There was nowhere to go but upward. Freedom waited. But no, the ceiling was in the way. And beyond the ceiling's high-wattage lighting fixtures and plain white tiles would come, I suspected, a formidable roof-ing structure. Wood and steel, bolts and nails and tar paper. But could these ordinary building materials really be obsta-cles? Already I was gaining elevation, and the world, as I saw it, was changing shape and form. The fact that I knew my liftoff to be an illusion—a cluster of persuasive somatic sensations expressing sexual fantasies as externalized visual and auditory distortions, to be exact—did not lessen the shock I felt when I looked down and saw my colleagues. These kind men and women, Manuel and Maria and Dan Graham and Sherwin Lang and Elizabeth Cole and, well, Peter Konwicki and his child psychologists, all these more or less friendly spectators were growing, to my eyes, smaller in size; they looked like people seen from an airplane ascending rapidly after its takeoff. But this is, I think, greatly reductive. To speak at all concisely about an hallucinatory episode is to risk the impression of something that might yield to intellection and the premeditated interventions of the Will. It is another matter altogether to realize, in that moment of flight from passion and from one's body—in that moment when your ears are loudly ringing and your stomach is doing its somersaults; when your friends and associates have turned suddenly and strangely into freakish dolls arranged around play-size tables; when your mouth has gone dry while your skin and clothes feel warmly damp all over; when your blood is racing while your heart in your chest beats so fiercely and so erratically that you fear it may fail; when you wonder, in other words, if this is how it feels to approach death, because it is conceivable that this is no ordinary anxiety attack, not at all, possibly this is something incredible and dreaded, something longed for and unstoppable and terribly, terribly final—it is another matter entirely to realize, when reflecting on rare nightmares like these, how weak and incomplete human intellection really is.

Here came the ceiling. I didn't dare look. I breathed the smells rising off Bernhardt, his shaving lotion and bad clothes, the man's rich scent of flowers dying in old water.

Was he hard?

As I grow older, I find that sexual excitation does not necessarily result in erection, per se, but in a roiling, washing, deep-in-the-pelvis warmth, as if the body has learned, over the years since adolescence and early manhood, to slow its responses, to suspend, dramatically, the sexual act and its completion, and instead remain, somewhat restfully, somewhat fitfully, in a condition of lovely, lingering anticipation. Then time decelerates, and this is a blessing. Those of us in middle or late age are by now familiar with the quickening hours, the faster and faster rushing past of days, months, the seasons of life. What's a year anymore? It is sex, I have found—*sex!*—or, more precisely, this state of being in awareness of sex, that gives a solid check against the clock, a countermeasure, in the brain, to the rapidity of the body's decline toward weakness, disease, senescence. If you think about what I am saying, if you concentrate on it, you will certainly recall, in your own experience, those precious moments that stand so alone in time: the glance across a room at the man or woman who will become the new lover: a kiss anticipated: the kiss.

The sun had descended outside and sex was everywhere around me. The kitchen doors swung open and a waitress, lit from behind by super-radiant, industrial-strength fluorescence, came through with a coffeepot in one hand and milk, one of those small stainless-steel creamers, held high before her in the other. She looked young; I flew down for a better view. Light spilled from kitchen to dining room, causing this waitress's medium-length skirt, as she entered, to become, briefly, translucent. Outlines of her legs showed. The girl's hair, ribboned, backlit, and fair, glowed in the light that framed her shadow thrown before her on the floor. I was not the only man watching the girl, her body in light. It was as if that light from the kitchen had been set up and aimed to capture this entrance with milk and coffee. Then the waitress, taking her time, admired by men, hesitated a moment while the swinging doors closed behind her. One door, then the next, on her left, then her right, clicked on its hinges, tipped shut. She did not look down or backward toward the doors. She stared ahead into the dining room and her shadow on the floor vanished as doors closed and there was no way to tell what she might have been thinking. Her dress reasserted itself and became opaque and plain around her. She knew where the doors were and she let them go and that ended our show.

"Tom."

"What?"

"Stop shaking."

It was Bernhardt speaking quietly to me, whispering kind words to make my fear go away. I grasped his hands tightly in mine. I was glad to be held. I felt that if set down, I might crumple over and fall from the heights and absolutely collapse. I said to the man, "Don't let go of me," and he promised, "I won't." Then Bernhardt hoisted me higher in his arms, a quick little lift as he tossed me around, shifting his own posture while readjusting the load—me, that is—in order to get better purchase, a more comfortable grip.

I can say in fairness that at that point, in that instant of being shaken around and arranged in Bernhardt's arms, I felt truly and strangely like a young child, myself as a child at, I would guess, roughly eighteen or twenty months in age. What I mean is that I *felt* the man's authority, his enormous strength. How did this come about? My own position, hoisted aloft in midair, was one of relative powerlessness. Yet this powerlessness, or helplessness, my lack of volition, my child-like perspective, whatever we want to call it, was in fact a complex state, in that it was not at all what it seemed; on the contrary, I was, in the ways that children can be, quite powerful, because I was free during those moments suspended in Bernhardt's arms, free to see the world as a place of my own making.

Richard Bernhardt, in spite of—because of—his most sinister qualities, his pressing, carnal threat, was doing a wonderful job accommodating my deepest longings and torments.

You see, that night at the Pancake House, perched high with feet hanging and my head rising upward to float closer and closer to the ceiling and lights, I felt, for a short while, as if I were becoming what every normal child most truly is: an inventor of reality.

I did what any average, middle-aged man might do in this situation. I tried to make eye contact with a mature woman.

I turned my gaze away from the youthful waitress standing so beautifully before the kitchen doors, away from other diners staring at this girl or huddled, more or less oblivious, in friendly alliances around square tables covered with blue cloths. The jukebox music played. There was talking and laughing, a quiet turmoil of noise made by people who looked and sounded as if they were pleased to be done with the day and out of the house. What were they all talking about? They appeared, my friends in their socioprofessional cliques, infatuated with one another. In particular there was, at one table, a great amount of interest in whatever Sherwin Lang was saying. Lang, like many alcoholics, is intelligent and a great pontificator; he is one of those lovely, well-preserved drunks whose talk is never boring and always—for reasons I can never quite pin down, though undoubtedly related to his sonorous, low-pitched speaking voice—always comforting. It is probably true that for some, the man's alcoholism makes him attractive; he has the bearing of a rake or a lost father, and naturally this causes women to fall precipitously in love with him. I have to admit that he is one of my favorite people. Tonight his table companions were listening intently to him, and who could blame them? "Take spaceships and unidentified flying objects," he was saying now over buckwheat pancakes and a bottled beer, his third or maybe fourth. "In my view, these are perfect instances of the phenomenon we're concerned with. What are spaceships if not ideal, visionary mislocations of human erotic desire? The existence or nonexistence of flying saucers is finally immaterial. Read Jung on this if you can stand reading Jung." He chuckled and let his companions acknowledge, with their own show of polite mirth, his preeminence as a thinker on matters relating to psychoanalytic doctrine and the canon; then he continued,

"What matters to the true believer are the structures of longing and paranoia surrounding the various controversies and all those, you know, those suspected conspiracies and whatnot that make up what passes for narrative in this issue. Neither saucers nor government cover-ups can be satisfactorily confirmed, and therefore the entire debate operates at the level of exciting metaphor."

"Dr. Lang, are you saying that people have UFO sightings as a substitute for working through their sexual hysterias?" The speaker was Leslie Constant, a third-year postdoctoral Institute trainee who had come to us from England, where she had grown disenchanted, understandably, with traditional British Object Relations Theory.

Sherwin drank from his beer, then went on in his accustomed manner of the scholarly dignitary granting an interview, "Well, not exactly, though I think it is pretty generally accepted that forbidden sexuality will express itself in complex, often frightening belief systems."

"Like religion?" prompted Leslie.

The table went quiet; it was possible that Leslie's question was too general, too obvious; was, in other words, a breach of academic decorum and restraint. Sherwin sipped again from his beer. His movements when he drank—the hand outstretched though clearly comfortable and relaxed, gliding along through space toward the glass bottle; and his long fingers showing, as his hand progressed toward the beer, their handsome nails; and then the fingers softly, gently, affectionately touching the dark glass, encircling and clasping it, *feeling* it; finally, hand and arm working together to raise, neither recklessly quickly nor conspicuously slowly, in other words not evidently self-consciously from an onlooker's point of view, the precious, all-important amber bottle—were movements made by a man intensely concentrated, at least whenever watched while drinking, on physical precision and the demonstration, acted out almost as a performance, of sobriety, dignity, and masculine beauty. He drank. The force of his personality was awesome. I have often surmised that this may have been a function less of his intellect than of his hair, swept back from the high forehead in a great black-and-gray mane that put one in mind of a nineteenth-century mathematician or poet-philosopher. His coat as well was cut in a style that looked antiquated somehow, snug at the waist and featuring narrow lapels riding out at severe angles from a four-button front that fully cloaked most of his exquisite wine-red tie. Sherwin's colleagues around the table nodded their heads while he told them, "Religion as ritualized communal orgasm—so much has been written on this. But, you know, religious practice is not primarily useful as a gateway to ecstatic states. Rapture is for the mystics and shamans and snake handlers, right? I think most observance is really more a way of conceptualizing day-to-day life as what it actually is for many people, a progress of meaningful failures."

"Do you really believe that, Sherwin?" It was Leslie Constant again, daring to speak Lang's Christian name and, in this way, assume a peer role and mildly undermine her supervisor's guru status—a potentially dangerous tactic with this man. He did nothing to show that he minded grilling by the trainee, perhaps because it was still early in the evening. Or maybe Leslie's English accent made her sound literate and shrewd. Sherwin regarded her with a look full of appreciation and, well, appetite—he smiled; and it was clear from his eyes, or I should say it was clear from Sherwin's decision to smile at Leslie in that generous, charming, menacing way he has, that the man enjoyed knowing the woman was in love with him.

"Sexual hysterias in general tend to manifest as social trends, and come and go in cycles." Sherwin was getting into teaching mode; once he has started, it can be hard to stop him. "In order to see this clearly, we have to reconsider the notion that psychological functioning shares the same growth curve as technological innovation. It is true that technology is one of the great expressions of the human spirit. As we all know, to be human is to make things. Bombs or poems or cures for diseases, what's important is making something. And if a thing *can* be made, it *must* be made!" At this point Sherwin placed his hand, open and with the palm facing downward, firmly on the tabletop; and the effect of this swift, almost unnoticeably subtle gesture, as he spoke, was a perfect demonstration of the man's total ability to orchestrate—much in the way that a symphony conductor at the podium will use his head and body and conductor's baton to organize the various musical strains into a seamless and singularly emotional, spectacular whole—the precise effects of his words on his listeners. Everyone at Sherwin's table leaned in close, and you could tell by looking at Leslie and Mike Breuer and Elizabeth Cole—Elizabeth so beautiful with her dark hair spilling over her ears—you could tell that for these three, the noises in the restaurant and all the miscellaneous activities and comings and goings of waitresses, all the busy distractions—including me up in Bernhardt's arms, watching the world, flapping insanely and kicking like a monstrous baby—these noises were, for the English trainee and the two clinical therapists sharing a pancake dinner with Sherwin, temporarily, profoundly out of awareness.

Lang carried on: "All that is neither here nor there except to say that technological and scientific advances are by definition inevitable, yet we are mistaken to expect spiritual or sexual awakenings as a result of breakthroughs in applied fields."

"You're saying that people are slow to assimilate to changes in the environment?" This was Elizabeth speaking. Hearing her, my heart pounded in my chest.

Sherwin also was affected by Elizabeth's voice. He made slow, easeful petting motions with his hand on the table, stroking the table, feeling, with his fingertips, the blue tablecloth; and he said, "The main point is that each generation thinks it has better sex than its parents, who had better sex than their parents. Right? As psychologists, we know that nothing could be further from the truth. But out in the culture, you know, people accept this on faith. Humans in their narcissism apparently must tell themselves that they live always on the verge of a bold new era in which shame and inhibition will be problems of the past."

"It's a way of defeating death!" Leslie blurted. She sounded, saying this, like a famous British film actress whose name I could not recall. Lang, amazingly—or maybe not amazingly—let her have the point.

"Yes, Leslie. That's right."

Then Leslie, encouraged to go on, raised her voice and said, with sudden, unexpected anger, "But that doesn't happen, does it? I mean, death comes and takes everything away."

"We know it does," said Lang softly to her. He was soothing her. The man and Leslie had reached, in that moment, some deep accord; they were, as people say, in sync. And something in the way each addressed the other made it possible to see that their conversation, that night at the Pancake House, was far from academic; rather, it was an intimate, encrypted courtship: Sherwin and Leslie, with help from Elizabeth and Mike as witnesses—these two accredited professionals standing in, symbolically, as the family that promises to support the "marrying" couple—were, in the space of a few brief statements, telling one another who they were and what they needed. Sherwin would take an educative role, the protector and guide into the fully adult, political world, a temporary father for the younger woman separated from home, orphaned and alone in a foreign country. Hadn't she just spoken openly and with feeling about death and loss? And hadn't he allowed her to speak her way toward her grief, then sanctioned her intelligence and her right to participate as a member of the psychotherapeutic community?

The tension around the table, pleasurable, electric, was rising. One had the feeling that Sherwin and Leslie might reach out and touch one another, hold hands like sweethearts. This didn't happen. Instead, after a hushed, suspenseful interval in which, I think, everyone watching had a chance to recognize the solemn significance of events taking place, Leslie said an amazing and revealing thing. It was one of those mysterious, unpremeditated bombshells people sometimes drop, whenever circumstances make it viable to declare, in a few puzzling, odd, possibly meaningless words, something of the essential and unifying personal logic known in our literature and our hearts as the Self.

Leslie turned and looked hard at Sherwin beside her. Her face was radiant. She gazed at her mentor the way a happy baby gazes at mother. "Maybe," declared this Englishwoman, "maybe sexual hunger should be described as the terror in love at the beginning of death."

Everyone had to think about that for a moment. Finally Mike Breuer realized that the time had come for him to perform his "official" symbolic function. I suppose Mike had been cautious, earlier, not to break in on whatever was happening between his colleague and the young woman. In any case, he now said, in a voice that sounded like the voice of a man offering a toast, "Whoa! That sounds damned good to me!" Everyone, including Sherwin, laughed, and the tension around the table was relieved in a completely pleasant way; and then Sherwin announced his answer to the woman who would become his lover: "We live in times of great hysteria. Death will save us."

This concluded, for the time being, Sherwin Lang's seduction of Leslie Constant. Lang's companions understood that important work had been done, understood the pitch and roll of Sherwin's voice, as he rattled off his last pronouncement, as a form of audible, dramatic cue, or coded instruction; accordingly, everyone at the table lowered his or her head and sat in silence. They were not unlike supplicants, praying.

I peered down, away from all these therapists under the

powerful spell of Sherwin Lang, down at my own messy table piled with coffee cups and horrible foods, our preposterous supper.

I looked to Maria. What I needed, I think, was some reality testing, as we are so fond of saying in this business.

Maria, incredibly—and somewhat rudely, I thought—was not paying attention to me. She was talking in subdued tones to the Kleinian beside her, Manuel Escobar.

"Look at me!" I cried at her. Was I very loud? Quiet? Had she heard? Would she care how I felt? I squirmed and thrashed in Bernhardt's arms. I got red in the face—I mean, my face felt hot—and my holder in his flopping panama hat complained, "Tom, take it easy, you're going to make me drop you on the floor. I can't hold you if you bounce around." Then Maria faced me and I noticed, as I do from time to time, how inviting she looked, her lips red and exquisite beneath bright lights.

I imagined kissing her or maybe nibbling a breast, and she said to me, "Tom, Manuel and I are having a conversation. Why must you always make problems for everyone?"

"I can't stop thinking about those afternoons we spent in the book and manuscript vault," I whispered to her, effectively acknowledging the pseudo-Oedipal triangle that consisted of this woman, Bernhardt, and me.

"You're ridiculous," Maria said. She wore a little smile, and I could see from this smile that she was, as I knew, a woman interested in pain, and that I still had a chance with her after all these years.

How pretty her hair looked, tugged back hard away from

her forehead and fastened behind her neck, severely clasped there. Maria's hair's different browns and occasional dyed-red strands ran together then spilled behind her shoulders.

"Meet me in the parking lot after dessert," I said, and immediately regretted it. What was dessert after a meal like ours? And she would never come to the parking lot. It was best to face facts. I'd have no luck with her. Meanwhile Bernhardt, if he and Maria were, as I imagined, in their love affair, Bernhardt would be enraged with me, jealous or at least concerned about his preeminence—therefore humiliated—whether Maria contrived to meet me or not.

And so it was. Richard's arms around my chest squeezed tighter. His breaths puffed and blew hard against my neck. He was upset, and the result was that once again I flew out of my manhandled body, up like a bird caught in a house, flapping over heads and too close to walls, unable to alight at windows that were, anyway, mostly shut.

How I wished I could've flown out a window and home. I admit it's a sentimental, weak idea; I have acknowledged already the awkward romanticism expressed in this kind of farfetched, escape-by-flight scenario, and can only say at this point, in my defense, that it was fast becoming the warm time of year, and that songbirds were returning north to lay eggs. You could hear them, all the migratory birds, the robins and the cardinals and the speckled whatevers, crying and chattering from the trees surrounding the Pancake House parking lot. And across town, at home, small trees and the flowering shrubs planted long ago by Jane had blossomed and were beginning again to show their first startling colors in advance of summer's deeper greens. It was April, and yellow tulips in a row before the fence out back had shot up to flower brightly while nights were still cold. Geraniums in a pot on the porch bloomed red. The Pritchetts' magnolia, partly shading their narrow, overplanted yard next door (Veronica Pritchett's unpleasant voice can always be heard, on warm evenings, reprimanding her husband, Sam, who cowers inside and leaves the gardening to her), reached branches across the high wooden fence and released petals gently onto our property, a half-moon of white underneath the tree's limbs.

Soon the nesting doves would appear, as they have each recent year, and settle on the windowsill beneath the air conditioner wedged into our bedroom window, the "window shaker," as appliance installation men refer to portable units like ours. There is a nook between sill and machine, broad and high enough for a nest. Our air conditioner gives yearly sanctuary to chicks, a protective ceiling against the hawks that circle on warm drafts rising from the flats along the river. Hatched baby doves flutter wings against the air conditioner's metal undercarriage, and this rapping made in June by feathers against steel is loud in the bedroom, even with the window shaker blowing on high.

Occasionally, hearing birds in the hour before light, Jane and I will wake, disturbed by babies.

"There they are," Jane might say in a way that sounds sleepily accusing or, perhaps—if I am already lying awake pondering birds, babies, and my own insufficiencies; if I am hearing her, in other words, through a filter of chagrin—mournful. Mournful over what? Birds?

"They're sweet," I might whisper in an effort to smooth over any subtextual roughness, any hard feelings that could threaten, so early in the morning, our happiness.

It never works to put out fires before the fires have caught. I am reminded of a Saturday morning at the house—this was not long ago, I think, though I will admit it gets harder and harder, these days, to be at all certain about time and its too rapid passing—when Jane marched into the bathroom while I was on the toilet. She said, "Tom, is there something I could be doing that I'm not, you know, doing?"

"What do you mean?"

"You know."

"No, I don't."

She shrugged and said, "In bed?"

"Sexually?"

"Yes. Sexually."

"I don't know. I don't think so, right offhand. Maybe. I don't know," I lied.

"Because you can tell me. You know that. If there's something I'm not doing. Sexually. That you would like."

"Well," I said, in order to shift attention away from me and politely hurry this conversation along—I was, as I have mentioned, sitting on the toilet, boxer shorts wrapped around my ankles—"Jane, is there something you want me to do for you?"

"That's not why I brought this up."

"I didn't say it was. I was only asking if maybe there is something new you want to try in bed, but you're reluctant to say what, or you don't exactly know what, and so you've asked me about me in order to find out, surreptitiously, about you."

I was nearing the point at which it would become impossible to hold in, any longer, what felt like an enormous shit on the way. I mention this only because it is true—*was* true, that cold morning as I sat on the toilet watching Jane leaning with hips against the sink, Jane staring down at her bare feet, her pretty toes on the icy bathroom floor—and not because I feel any extraordinary interest in scatology or the bodily mechanics of defecation. Naturally I realize that much has been written, in my profession, on the intimate relationship between feces and neuroses. It is not, however, in either an academic or a clinical spirit that I confess my discomfort in the bathroom with Jane leaning back talking about love. I said to her, "Honey, if you're uncomfortable asking for something, you may be imagining desire as something located inside me, in order to relieve your own tension and make me the container for your erotic fantasies."

"Can't you leave that stuff at the office, Tom?"

"Seriously, Jane. You started this conversation, I didn't," I said, petulantly, and felt the beginnings of the bowel movement. Jane shifted her weight, pulled her robe tightly around her waist, then resettled herself against the wall behind her back and the sink rim beside her. I felt embarrassed. Certainly there is nothing attractive about an unshaved man on the toilet in the morning. Actually, Jane likes to watch me pee; she says it looks friendly—that's her word, and I appreciate the sentiment behind it. Usually, though, Jane doesn't hang around when I'm about to crap, and I extend her the same courtesy; in this respect we are probably like most sensible couples who plan to stay together over time. We respect one another's shame. Let me say in this light that I take no special pleasure in reporting on my bowel movements, and would not do so for one minute were it not for the fact that Jane was showing no sign of leaving the bathroom. In the meantime I was chattering and pontificating, loudly, to cover the unromantic, humbling sound of shit hitting the water. "It is not unusual," I announced from the toilet, "to invest other people with precisely those qualities or feelings that we most wish we did not ourselves possess, qualities and feelings that we have not learned to accept or even recognize in ourselves." Splash. "A great deal of antisocial pathology is actually a consequence of this tendency to search out and find the most discomfiting aspects of ourselves in other people, frequently the people closest to us." Splash. "We then feel permission to criticize these bad others, conveniently throwing off our own psychosexual confusion and self-loathing in the process"—plop, splash—"thereby symbolically aligning ourselves, like good children in a bad family, with the culture of blame and deceit."

Time to wipe. Jane smiled down at me in familiar, indulgent pity. As usual, she regarded my casual theorizing as a flight, a defense of fragile intellect against vital emotions, the male versus the female principle; as an attempt, in other words, to block or at least circumvent the kind of deep and destabilizing encounter that feels like, for want of a better word, connection. With one hand she fiddled with her bathrobe's sash, its bowed knot. I, done on the toilet, reached back to flip the lever and flush. Was Jane, discussing sexuality in the bathroom while her husband shat, expressing libidinous wishes? I tugged up boxers. The smell of shit, that warm bathroom smell, was in the air. It was too cold outside to open a window. I am not, as a rule, a morning-sex enthusiast, though on this morning I felt, suddenly, great hopefulness and a new sense of life's splendid possibilities. The sun's rays came through high clouds to light the world outside. Humidity was low. It was Saturday, the weekend, and it occurred to me that all my problems at the Institute were inconsequential, ephemeral. Those annoying child psychologists, Peter Konwicki and his gang, those psychosocial bureaucrats couldn't pester me about my Young Women of Strength program. I never hear Peter and his merry men contributing brilliant insights at the Young Women of Strength outreach meetings. They lean back in their chairs and they cross their legs, and every now and again one will pipe up, "Tom, how do you plan to explain to Sheryl Babcock's mother that Sheryl has left home on your advice to pursue a tap-dancing career?" or "Tom, do you think it's a good idea to make 'Famous Hippies and Visionary Dropouts' the theme of the next social?"

Jane was not leaving her place beside the sink. This meant I had to wash my hands. If I walked out of the bathroom without washing, Jane might become distressed. It would be interesting to do a study on bathroom hand-washing patterns among couples at different stages in their marriages. I padded over, stood before the sink, gazed in the mirror at my skinny body wearing underwear, and felt sad. I don't have much hair left, except on my extremities and, lightly here and there, on my stomach and chest. The hair on my head looks awful, spare and patchy, like some weeds left standing in a field after a bad winter. Tiny gray hairs stuck out from my ears. When in the recent years did these begin to show? And a number of new moles had appeared—*when? when did my body begin to transform itself into an old man's body?*—various dark spots scattered high and low, my own miniature pointillist seascape, the body's self-made tattoos taking shape across chest and shoulders.

Mostly I regret not exercising more regularly. Jane says I look sweet. But my eyes, as I grow older, look as if they have sunk; they're ringed with dark, unbecoming circles, and are often bloodshot.

Jane in repose against the sink turned her head and faced the mirror. Our eyes peered into the glass. It was unsettling to see Jane this way, in profile and so close, my Jane and the Jane reflected in the medicine cabinet mirror, the touchable woman looking away and her image looking toward me, watching me watch myself watching her and her reflection. Jane's head was tilted. Her face wore a smile, though not much of one. Jane's eyes looked, actually, as if they were staring at something behind me—at trees and the clouds outside our bathroom window? Her expression was one you might describe, because of its stillness, as a meaningful absence of expression, as expressive inexpressiveness, and it meant, I thought, that Jane was waiting for me to tell her what I wanted in bed. I reached for soap in its dish and this brought my hand close to Jane's hip propped against the sink rim. I picked up the soap and turned on the tap and began scrubbing madly. Jane and I and our two reflections paid attention. I put on a display of getting clean. This may or may not have been in response to Jane's seductiveness. The bathroom in morning light, tiled white all around, seemed like a large area, though it is not. The sink is beside the doorway, and Jane, stationed beside the sink, blocked the door.

"What do you want from me?" I scoured my hands. I did not intend my question to sound threatening or suspicious. I looked into the mirror and could see, along with Jane's eyes there, bathroom walls and a section of window behind me. Sun, a faint yellow light, broke through the clouds; immediately the room brightened and the mirror took on glare, a halo around Jane's reflected face. Outside, clouds raced above the treetops—in, then out of, the bathroom window's frame, in, then out of, the mirror's glass. Morning light came and went, obscuring Jane's reflected smile.

"Relax, Tom."

"I'm relaxed." Water from the tap ran hot and I saw that my hands were red from heat and excessive washing. I turned up the cold, and Jane said, "You don't look relaxed."

"You're right."

"What can I do?" Jane asked me. In this way we came full circle to her original question. Jane's voice sounded full of caring and tenderness. But, as we all know, people wishing to extract intimate intelligence will often adopt a gentle demeanor. Jane is expert at inviting and permitting, in another person, the kinds of mood states required for disclosure and confession of even the most galling, humiliating experiences and feelings. There is nothing more seductive—and dangerous—than being listened to.

I dried my hands on a towel. My hands felt chapped and

raw. The floor was cold. I said, "I need a cup of coffee. If you want, we can talk about painting the little room."

"Oh, Tom."

"I mean it. We'll go through the color samples and make preliminary choices. I'll drive to the hardware store later and get spackling compound. We'll need lots, I guess."

Was I crazy? Why bring this up? What might happen to me and Jane, how might our lives change forever, if we fixed up the room at the head of the stairs? Or, to ask this question differently, what are the possible uses, in a childless house, of an empty room? Let's assume, for discussion purposes, that the room remains unused, its door unopened, its broken walls unpainted and the unclean windows securely locked. Nothing gets put in the room, and nothing can come out. The room functions symbolically as a container for anything that is imagined, hoped for, dreamed about. If the room is a baby's room, then it is a baby's room missing a baby, and this of course is another way of saying that the room contains loss. The room is not empty, exactly; something unseen lives inside.

"Are you sure this is a good idea?" asked Jane.

"I thought you wanted to."

"I did."

"You did?"

"I just don't know if there's any point, Tom."

"There's no reason to leave the room empty forever," I said; and realized, saying this, that there were any number of good and less good reasons to do exactly that. Jane, I felt, understood this. Hatred was in the look she gave me when she turned away from the bathroom mirror. She pulled her robe tightly around her.

"What?" I said.

"Are you sleeping with Maria?"

"Sleeping with Maria?"

"Are you?"

"No."

"Did you ever?"

"Why are you asking me this, Jane?" And I thought, then, of Manuel. Was Jane asking about Maria because she had begun sleeping with Escobar, because she needed, in order not to part from me, an even playing field, the impression of symmetry between us?

"Does that mean yes?" she asked.

"No, it doesn't."

"Can you answer the question?"

"Yes."

"Yes, you can answer the question, or yes, you made love to Maria?"

"I didn't make love to Maria."

"You fucked her."

"What do you mean by 'fuck,' exactly?" I said, stupidly. This was a defensive move, though not purely defensive. I suppose I had it in mind to act on the principle, controversial among some, that admission of infidelity, more perhaps than the infidelity itself, is a violation of the marriage vows, and that any evasiveness during confrontations over fidelity and trust, however dishonorable this evasiveness might be in theory, can in reality be seen as a generous and noble strategy.

Jane apparently was not in a mood to consider the destructive effects of confessional revelations. "Were we married?"

"I don't remember."

"Bullshit."

"Jane."

"What?"

"Jane, Jane," I said that morning as she turned away from me and walked out of the bathroom.

She did not go into our bedroom; she avoided the bedroom and passed barefoot along the upstairs hall toward the stairs. I went after her, whispering, "Jane, Jane."

She didn't go downstairs. The room at the head of the stairs was on her left. The cat sat on the stairs, two or three steps down, and I could see the cat's head and white whiskers and pointed ears above floor level, sticking up. Jane put her hand on the little room's doorknob, turned the knob, and opened the door. She went in.

I went in.

Next the cat came in.

I left the door open. On second thought, I closed it.

We were all in the room. The windows faced north. Outside was our front yard, cut in half by the drive leading away from the house, winding through trees to the road that takes you across the river to town. Bright light came through the clouds, faded then came again. The room remained dark. Plaster walls showed holes where shelves or pictures hung once. Some other family had, a long time before, used this room for something, then left and taken everything away. Dirt and dead insects were on windowsills and in corners on the floor. Had someone swept the insects into the corners? A moth near the ceiling flew. How had a moth gotten in past locked windows?

The cat saw the moth and focused on it. The cat stayed still, but her head moved, her eyes moved, following the moth's erratic flight. Dust on the floor was thick and showed paw prints and Jane's naked footprints leading to the place where Jane stood with her back facing me. The sun broke through the clouds and cobwebs became visible against the windowpanes, silhouetted. The room was full of living and dead things. Jane untied her bathrobe's sash and, just like that, the robe dropped off her shoulders and down her back into a pile of blue cloth around her feet.

I am a lucky man.

I saw those Winslow Homer moles on Jane's back. "Hello, baby," Jane said to the cat near her feet. The cat forgot the moth and rubbed itself against Jane's legs, and Jane leaned over to pet her head. There was Jane's ass. The cat located the moth again and leaped to a windowsill to get closer to the ceiling. The cat is female but we call her Larry, after Lawrence Mandelbaum, my analyst and the father of Self / Other Friction Theory. The name Lawrence was my mistake when the cat was a kitten. The kitten turned out to be a girl, but Lawrence stuck and Larry's her name. She watched her moth until the moth landed on the ceiling and she lost interest and looked at me. Jane, I thought, expected me to know what to do. I didn't know what to do. Or I should say that I knew some things to do, but not how to begin. Relationships go in phases and there are moments in them that mark the close of one phase and the start of another. Usually these moments are small and pass without anyone realizing, until later, that something momentous was contained in an offhand remark or a shrug, a little laugh maybe, when nothing very funny had been said. The moment passes, but the cool remark, the indifferent gesture, the cryptic laugh has done its transformative work. Most people, I am sure, will know exactly what I am referring to—those small scenes in a marriage or friendship that become, in memory, incidents, reverberant with dark meaning. It is best, in a way, when these moments pass in silence, because they can then be recalled and talked about. But if, in the moment when big changes are taking place, if you are awake to what is happening, then gentle conversation is out of the question.

"I'm sorry," I said.

"Shut up," Jane said.

She was naked, with her back to me. She said, "You still haven't answered my question."

There were, at this point, I felt, too many questions, the questions leading to new questions. And of course I had my own questions, and no clear way to ask them.

"Which question, Jane?"

"Please don't say my name right now. You can't say my name now. I don't want you to say my name."

"Which question?"

"The question about what you want me to do."

"You should do what you want, I guess."

"I asked what *you* want, Tom. What do you want me to do? Do you want me to fuck you?"

"Oh, God."

"I can do that. I can fuck you with a dildo or I can fuck you with my hand."

The moth fluttered down from the ceiling and the cat jumped off the windowsill, stalking. She sat on her hind legs and watched, and muscles in her back twitched. Then the moth flew over and Larry sprang up with paws batting the air. The moth was high and she missed. It was a little white moth. Jane said, "Come here."

Did she mean me or the cat? I did what she said. I moved up behind her. So did the cat. The cat moved this way and that between our legs as, on Jane's back, the wave shapes rose and fell, tossing the men and spraying mist, Jane's tiny birthmarks scattered across the skin.

The room with its windows closed felt cold and airless, somewhat like an attic in winter. Sounds outside, the wind through trees and so on, were hardly audible. There was space for a bed and a table, a chest of drawers, not much else. I had goose bumps.

We were sealed in tight. The city and the Institute, and the hospital and the river and the road, and our yard and even other rooms in our house were far away. The world was far away. Or, looked at from another, more imperious, narcissistic perspective, the world was in the room. The cat made a noise and Jane said, "Put your arms around me."

There was tenderness. I felt, holding Jane, that everything would be all right as long as we remained together in the room—an impossibility, past a certain point, and therefore an entirely sentimental notion. Or maybe not. Relationships are like powerful moods that people share. We can go a little mad in our love relationships. Jane and I have always had what I would call a good love, in that it has been possible to go mad, but never too mad; in other words, we do not, when falling in and out of love, fall too far away from, or too profoundly into, the world.

Now a peculiar, gentle animosity was growing between us. I felt that we loved one another, and peace was in the little room. What waited outside? I held Jane and felt her stomach, the bottom of her rib cage, the skin above her hips. Her hair was in my face. The air was cold and the floor felt cold to the touch. My hands touching Jane were icy; she flinched and pressed her back against my chest.

The cat ran after the moth flying in circles near the ceiling. I watched the moth in flight. The cat rolled on the floor and came up dirty. Jane's hair was in my mouth. I could hear the wind outside, and Jane's breathing, and my own. I studied her back and saw freckles dotting Jane's shoulders like stars above the sea on her hips. Below Jane's neck, on a place usually hidden beneath her hair, I saw, I think, the Little Dipper.

We pulled each other down onto the floor. The cat got between us and curled up for warmth. I had the beginnings of a cold. Jane, making love, has such poise. We weren't kissing. In the middle of everything, Jane began talking. She talked and talked, for the longest time, and it was fantastic to hear her. I kept my mouth shut. I breathed and listened. She said, "I used to love you so much, Tom. It was a simple thing, loving you. I didn't worry about us loving other people. I thought about that, the possibility, but I never worried. I thought I could care for somebody else and still love you. It didn't seem like a problem. You know? Why wouldn't we love other people? Loving other people isn't bad. But it's wrong to think that everything won't change. You feel like a different person when you make love with someone new. Falling in love with a new person is a way of becoming a new person. Well, not a new person. A different version of yourself. It's true. That's the wonderful part, and it's the difficulty too, I suppose. I don't want you to be a new person. I always want you to be the man I fell in love with, but that's stupid, because I'm not the girl you fell in love with. We're different people and we haven't kept track of who we are. That's why we're in this room, isn't it? This is where we can come to find out who we want to be when things change and we feel strange to each other. I think we each have versions of ourselves that we don't know are in us. Are you scared? Don't be. You're a man and I'm not a girl. Do you remember how young we used to be? We were so young in our twenties. We were children. I was riding that enormous, man's bike I used to have, remember? It was about a million billion sizes too big for me, and I was riding on the sidewalk, which you're not supposed to do, and then there you were in front of me and I ran into you. Well, I guess I didn't run into you, did I? You jumped out of the way. What happened? You tripped over that hedge, and that dog came tearing out of the yard on the hill. God. The dog's owner ran after the dog and yelled at us to leave his dog alone and get the hell off his property. All of a sudden, because of that man and his dog, we were united. We were a couple. Think of the ways people meet! I got off my bike and it felt like, 'Oh, hello.' We walked together, and you were sweet and took my bike and walked it for me, and we weren't paying any attention to where we were going, and the next thing we knew it was nighttime and we were in that scary part of town where the book factory is, so we went into that bar, remember, but we didn't drink anything, did we? We ordered club soda, and the bartender turned out to be the father of a kid who beat you up in high school, then later got killed in that terrible loading-dock accident. The father wouldn't stop talking about how death was everywhere, and he got impatient with us for drinking club soda, and we gave him a huge tip, because of his dead son, and just to get out of there. We went right to bed, that night, didn't we? I was afraid to take off my clothes. You kissed my back and told me it was beautiful, my back. I believed you. Do you ever want to be a different kind of man? Could you be a different man with a different woman if I were the woman? Don't be hurt, don't take it personally. Who else did you fuck, anyway? Tom? Actually, do you want me to tell you something? I'm not sure I want you to say. How would you feel about that? Would you think I don't care? Can you fuck me like I'm all the people you might ever love? Why am I telling you not to be hurt? It's because I want to fuck like I'm everybody and not just me. Is that a crazy thing to want?"

"Nothing is crazy," I said, though I know otherwise from my job. It was unclear whether she needed an answer from me. She said, "The cat's in the way. Move the cat, will you?" And, to the cat, "Sorry, honey, you have to go over there now." Then, to me, "She's sweet, isn't she?" Next she spoke to the cat again. "Hey, are you going to catch your white moth, sweetheart?" After a moment she whispered to me, "Look, she's watching us. Don't slow down, okay? We can fuck in front of Larry, she doesn't care. Pull the bathrobe over us, will you? It's cold in here. I like this room, I think. The floor is filthy, isn't it? It's pretty, the way the light is bright outside but doesn't shine directly in. It's so blue out, Tom. The days are getting longer. Have you noticed?"

"Yes."

I had a runny nose and nothing to wipe my nose with except Jane's bathrobe. I used her bathrobe's sash as a handkerchief. I was careful not to let Jane see me doing this. She said, "Soon we'll turn the clocks forward. It'll get windy and rainy, and you'll be depressed."

"I will?"

"You always are in spring. You know that. The tulips come up and the Pritchetts' magnolia blooms, and it stays cold for a long time, and then Easter comes, and after that you get depressed, and later it gets warm and the mourning doves come."

"Doves," I said.

"They make their nest in the window," Jane said; and she asked, "How many years have they been coming?" Then she explained, "They make homes out of whatever they find, broken sticks and copper wire and dirty string and rubber bands and tape."

All this time, while Jane and I talked, we were making love. Jane quietly cried and I held her head in my hands. She said, "Do you mind my hand? It hurts a little if I push? Can I push harder into you?"

"If you want."

"But what do *you* want?" she asked; and she told me, "You're a man and I'm not a girl and I'm not who you think I am, you shit."

After that, in the little room, for a little while, as sunlight came and went, we cried and fucked.

It was not yet the season, that April night at the Pancake House, for nesting doves to fly north and make homes beneath bedroom air conditioners. Frost coated leaves and the grass on these early spring mornings. Some days felt summery when the sun came up; others were winter-dreary, and on the bleak days it looked like a late, last snow might fall from the white sky.

As it happened, that evening at the restaurant, spring's heavy rains were on the way. I could tell from changes in my mood. Coming rainfall—the spattering drops that blow in from a distance, out from dark weather advancing over the horizon, blotting out the daytime sun or the Milky Way at night—invariably causes me to feel irritable and worried. Confusion sets in, or a mild fretfulness, really, that grows and intensifies as, from the north or northwest, precipitation advances. Then I become withdrawn, on a sunless day or muggy night, and fall into a mood of quiet trepidation that may, I believe, have its natural analogue in the wary stillness adopted by forest animals during the hours preceding a storm. What is more quiet than that silence heard from skunks and raccoons before a downpour? It follows that anticipation of rainfall engenders, in humans, sensations that could truly be called primordial and atavistic—those old and, in modern urban life, often scarcely perceived terrors of the dark, of isolation and the cold, hunger and loneliness and death from starvation or some other outcome of exposure; the unanalyzable terrors, best articulated not in language, rather by the body's tense, speechless postures of watchfulness and dread.

What I am trying to say is that I was in a panic, that hazy night at the Pancake House & Bar, as I floated up from Bernhardt's arms—one foot, then two, finally three feet into the air above our table. I glanced down at my friends around other tables, Elizabeth and Sherwin, Peter and Dan, Terry and Mike, Maria and Manuel, and Leslie and the other trainees, the whole relational matrix, and I felt, seeing their faces, queasier and queasier—it was like a case of drunken spins. In my practice I work with men and women recovering from addictions, and I am always fascinated by their descriptions of withdrawal, particularly the typically awful booze withdrawal featuring its pornographic hallucinations of multitudinous crawling bugs, devouring serpents, and freakish, hairy toads. Looking down at my colleagues around their dollhouse tables, I felt in sympathy with the addict; these women and men, my dear coworkers in their chairs below me, were, to my mind, a menacing, buggy swarm—a deadly hive of analysts wearing caked-on makeup and beady eyeglasses and cardigan sweaters knit from wool like matted fur.

Naturally I tried flying away. The world outside the restaurant waited. Jane waited, and home waited. But flying was not easy; it was not a matter of flapping my arms, veering left or right, turning somersaults in the air or darting back and forth to light on windowsills or countertops before leaping again to glide above the houses and the hills, away from all these people with snarling faces, away from problems and straight up, headlong over the book factory and the covered bridge, out past the burial mound, following the river into the chilly night.

I couldn't flap my arms. They were pinned to my sides by Bernhardt's. How had I managed to get in such a bind over a stack of cinnamon-raisin toast? If I flew away, if I truly flew, would Bernhardt accompany me? Might Bernhardt, this obese and lumbering man, remain attached, riding along with me from place to place, piggyback? It was a gruesome possibility. As always, I could feel the man's breath on my cheek. You could say that Bernhardt's presence was becoming a constant in my life. Waving my arms was impossible, really. I had no wings! I kicked my feet as a flight test and Bernhardt punished me for this with a mild squeeze to the ribs. The reasons to fly were both physical and psychological. In other words, flying would be a sexual act, and consequently hazardous.

Maybe if I closed my eyes. But no, this was bad. It is helpful, when nauseated from rocking and swaying, to focus on a still point in the distance—a lighthouse, for instance, if there is one in view. I looked out a nearby window. And there it was. There was the municipal hospital with its brightly lighted roof built in the shape of an Egyptian pyramid. This roof stood out against the fogged-up sky; it glowed above the slate black, steel-and-glass tower supporting it. The tower itself was almost invisible in the night, and the hospital's upper stories—missing, in the fog, their otherwise visible support, the massive building underneath—hovered over the business district and the old, polluted riverfront. This floating pyramid was, obviously, an illusion; but it was a lovely, appealing one. The roof looked, to me, gazing at it from far off, through the low, wet mist gathering in advance of rain—the hospital's pyramidal top looked as if it were levitating, a shining temple floating fifteen stories high.

Had the architects known how their building would appear at night? Did the hospital's planners conceive this effect of a great Egyptian burial chamber, a holy resting place in the sky above our city?

I kept my eye on the pyramid. As I have noted, the main part of the hospital building, the dark, perpendicular rectangle beneath the pyramid, had more or less vanished in the mist. Operating rooms; the nurses' stations and waiting areas for family and friends; the blood and pathology laboratories, the pharmacy and the morgue; and echoing corridors, the long halls leading to identical rooms furnished with new beds for sick patients—these things, it seemed to me as I looked out the restaurant window, were gone. All that was left was the roof. What did those top floors contain? The intensive care unit? The maternity ward? The most expensive, private rooms? Thunder rumbled, though only faintly; the storm remained miles to the north. The hospital pyramid, hanging over the city, looked as if it might blast off and depart into space. Or might it instead plop down and settle on the ground—maybe on one of the Kernberg College playing fields or, more likely, at a safe distance outside town, not far from the Pancake House, on one of the unused airport's broken landing strips, where the hobbyists fly their wood-and-paper planes?

"Look," I whispered to the man holding me.

"What?"

"The hospital."

"What about it?"

"It's a spaceship."

Bernhardt scolded, "Tom, knock it off. The hospital is not a spaceship."

"Ask Manuel if you don't believe me," I said, then asked Manuel myself. "Escobar, is the hospital a spaceship?"

The Kleinian gazed out the window at the building in the clouds. He was thinking. Finally he answered, "Yes."

It was as if Manuel's saying this made it true. No one spoke for a moment; we all peered out the window above the booth, Maria and Manuel, Richard and I; and the mist rolled in and thunder sounded again; and suddenly I felt myself shooting up into the air—absolutely up and away, around and around beneath the ceiling's grimy white tiles, without even trying.

Lights flew past. Or, more accurately, I flew past the lights, barely missing most. Looking down, I could see the people in the room looking up, watching me learn to fly. I cruised over Sherwin Lang and Sherwin saw me and smiled, and this pleased me, and for an instant I forgot to pay attention and nearly banged into a decorative cast-iron skillet hanging from a hook over the child psychologists. I did a little dip and roll around the skillet, and the psychologists all ducked. I saw Elizabeth Cole at three o'clock. The lights near the ceiling were exceptionally bright and hot. Below me was the fish tank. I made a mental note to swoop down and snag, from a table, any table, toast or a muffin, then circle back and dive-bomb the child psychologists. Elizabeth waved and I lost her in the lights and had to look away, and this almost caused another accident when Dan Graham got up to go to the men's room. Dan is a heavy man with a long beard; he looked, that night, in his flannel shirt and jeans and orthopedic shoes, as if he could hurt you in a fight. In fact, Dan is an avid rider of Harley-Davidson motorcycles. It is always interesting to observe the ways people style themselves to fit the roles suggested by their passions and hobbies. Dan with his tied-back hair and his thick arms and huge gut walked—limped, actually; the man's right leg was significantly shorter than his left, necessitating the special shoes—Dan limped directly into my path, and it was luck more than skill when I sheared hard to the right past his head and straight toward Maria, the only person in the restaurant able to make me feel safe and loved. It would have been heavenly to drop into Maria's arms; but this was not to be. The kitchen doors opened, spilling light from behind, and out came our waitress, our beautiful Rebecca, carrying water glasses on a metal tray. Rebecca set out between the crowded tables. Everything was fine until Sherwin signaled for a waitress, and Rebecca, seeing him, picked up speed. I was certainly going to fly straight into her. I would not have minded this if it had not been for the water glasses and the likelihood of a noisy accident. In fact, Rebecca was probably accustomed to boys her age concocting awkward excuses to barge into her—the old adolescent game of sexual touching disguised as rough, schoolyard teasing and playing. However, it would not be right for me, a grown man occupying a position of so-called responsibility in the commur.ity, to mow down a high-school girl making money for college. It'd be nice at least to zoom in close and smell her hair. What could be wrong with that? She was not far, only three or four short steps, from Lang. The child psychologists watched her saunter by their table; and it was obvious that Konwicki, in particular, was checking out her ass. But who could blame the man? Rebecca looked good—no, *fantastic*—in her waitress's uniform. The uniform itself was, unfortunately (or fortunately, depending on one's preferences in women's fashions), quite prim: blue gingham dress coyly hemmed above pretty knees; billowing sleeves finished with lace cuffs buttoned at the wrists; a high lace collar above white clasps running up (or trailing *down;* again, a great deal depends on how you see these things) the front. You can't expect waitresses wearing miniskirts and black tights at a pancake restaurant. I, for one, am charmed by the theater of supposed innocence, and have no objection to drab costumes on females. What is more beautiful than beauty unveiled? Who can honestly deny the urge to breach a virtuous façade?

Here Rebecca came. We were on our collision course. I wanted to tackle her and get tangled up in her clothes. The realization of this desire made me wiggle and shake. Did Bernhardt notice this? Would he mind? Dan Graham lumbered out of the men's room, and Rebecca stopped suddenly to let him pass. Rebecca's waiting gave me an opportunity to fly by without adjusting altitude. Dan made his way to his chair and I missed Rebecca by inches, then buzzed over Sherwin Lang for the second or maybe third time that night. "What was that?" Leslie Constant's English-accented voice said, as I screamed past the fish tank and nearly smashed into a window overlooking the parking lot.

I was not, at this point, making a very good showing as a flying man. I might have done better if I had not eaten the pancakes. We eat pancakes to escape loneliness, yet within moments we want nothing more than our freedom from ever having so much as thought about pancakes. Nothing can prevent us, after eating pancakes, from feeling the most awful regret. After eating pancakes, our great mission in life becomes the repudiation of the pancakes and everything served along with them, the bacon and the syrup and the sausage and coffee and jellies and jams. But these things are beneath mention, compared with the pancakes themselves. It is the pancake—*Pancakes! Pancakes!*—that we never learn to respect. We promise ourselves that we will know better, next time, than to order pancakes in any size or in any amount. Never again will we be tempted by buckwheat or buttermilk or blueberry flapjacks. However, we fail to learn; and the days go by, two or three weeks pass, then a month, and we forget about pancakes and their dominion over us. Eventually, we need them. We crawl back to pancakes again and again.

I slumped, midair, against the window frame. Outside were cars parked in the lot. The night beneath approaching rain clouds was black beyond reach of the restaurant's outdoor lights. Mist turned to thicker fog, covering cars. The cars in the light glowed beneath the gray, obscuring fog; they seemed, somehow, these cars, to glow and vanish at the same time. Tires on the ground were invisible, though bumpers, hoods, and windshields shimmered in the wet air. Nothing much could be seen beyond the last row of automobiles. Tree trunks. A patch of brown grass. The electric outdoor light dissipated in mist, and colors on faraway cars were muted and indistinguishable. The car bodies were wet hulks. I could see, close to the restaurant building, Maria's yellow sports coupe parked beside Bernhardt's red station wagon. Bernhardt's red wagon became purple in the dull light. This car was a flagship; others behind and around it looked small and vulnerable. I could not help feeling sad for the cars.

My own car, my little green sedan, was not in the lot, because Jane had driven me here and dropped me off.

I felt sick and alone, looking out at cars and eavesdropping on the child psychologists, whose voices were so loud.

"He's borderline. I'm sure of it," said Peter Konwicki to the man beside him, an earnest, irritating trainee named Bob. Bob nodded his head and Konwicki said, "I don't like to diagnose my coworkers, but in this case I'm willing to make an exception."

"Would you say that he is a multiple?" asked Bob in his eager, ingratiating way—trying, I guess, to score points with Konwicki.

These two men stared at me for a moment, and Peter was clearly—how shall I say this?—disgusted. Finally he pronounced, "Contrary to popular belief, Bob, full-fledged multiple personalities are extremely rare, and should not be confused with personalities that are merely fragile and poorly defended, like chronic depressives and substance abusers who never manage to become adequately socially integrated. Those people typically conceive grandiose characters and world views, and then suffer tremendous psychic stress when the world around them fails, as it always must in the end, to honor or reward their solipsism. Our colleague is somewhat like that, I would say. But is he a true multiple? No, he's something else."

"Manic?"

"Possible manic tendencies, yes."

"Schizoid?" asked the child-psych trainee, excited.

"There's a fair chance of that."

"Paranoid?"

"Paranoid, oh yes, without a doubt," said Konwicki. This apparently was Bob's cue to go into a kind of frantic seizure, rocking in his chair and making jerky, disturbing hand and arm movements, wild gestures that indicated a crisis of agitation and made me think of rabies.

"Winnicottian false self? Delusional fantasies of power and omniscience? Sexual deviancies?" shouted Bob like a maniac.

"I wouldn't rule anything out, Bob."

"Fantastic!"

One thing was certain: Peter and I were headed for an altercation of one sort or another. Maybe not tonight, but sometime before long. I was sure of it. I don't want to say that I was hoping for something physical, because I am not a brawler and have no wish—that I know of—to harm another person or, alternatively, get roughed up myself. It could be problematic, too, to enter a fighting contest while being lofted in the air by another man. Kicking would be an option. Maybe Bernhardt, with his skin the color of canned salmon and his wrinkled red coat and that panama hat that never—as I think I have already mentioned, maybe more than once—comes off his head in public, so that one imagines him wearing it in the most absurd and private places as well, in his morning shower or beside his wife in bed at night, or even at the barber, who would, one imagines, snip gingerly at the stiff little hairs that find their way out from beneath the horrible hat (or, uglier yet, one pictures the hat as a kind of drooping straw covering for some lurid and unsightly growth or deformity on the top of Bernhardt's head, a medical anomaly, or, ghastlier even than this, some moist, translucent parasite from the pages of science fiction, an alien thing planted on Bernhardt, living on him and connected, through the central nervous system, to his brain, controlling him and instructing him, via little tubes, to hold me and squeeze me and teach me to fly; instructing him, as well, to deny that the hospital in the mist is a spaceship or, more beautifully and more to the point, a golden, floating tomb)—maybe Bernhardt, as I was saying, Bernhardt, our giant, wheezing, pink-cheeked Group counselor, would appear, to Konwicki, intimidating. Konwicki is a little guy. He looks scrappy and angry and mean and tough. But it is well known that these feral men with their pressed-together lips and narrow eyes set beneath shiny foreheads, these men who look squirrelly and aggressive, with veins showing on forearms and biceps, men who seem perpetually hungry and absolutely resentful about everything good in life—these types, I have found, will show themselves to be submissive or at least wildly avoidant in moments of true conflict or threat from a big, fat, food-obsessed male.

This was my hope in the event of a battle for eminence, that night. In the meantime I could feel Bernhardt's body pressing harder against mine. I mean I could feel, at points along the length of me, Bernhardt's stomach and his legs and, there against the small of my back, what must have been his cock. Or was it his leather belt, or his bunched-up jacket, pushing against my back at the base of my spine? Feeling this, I came also to feel as if each part of Bernhardt, his legs and his arms and his chest and, from time to time, his abrasive, slightly blotchy chin nestling against the back of my head (all this taken together making up what you might call the length and breadth of Bernhardt)—I came to feel, as I was saying, as if each part of this man were touching each part of me, my legs and my arms and my stomach and ribs encircled by Bernhardt's arms holding me off the floor. And then, on further consideration of these feelings brought about by the closeness of Bernhardt, his legs and belly pressing against me, these feelings brought *through* Bernhardt's body into my own—on further consideration I came to feel, as the two of us stood still in our big, never-ending hug, breathing in time with one another while hardly daring to move, I came to feel like the man was no longer behind me; rather, he was lying on top of me, crushing me, I down on my stomach and he on his stomach, sprawled across my back, with his whole huge weight bearing down and his breath drifting sweetly through the air around my face, Richard's breath tickling, rhythmically, metronomically, with each warm exhalation, the hairs on my ears, those almost undetectable hairs that stick out absurdly, the hairs of a man growing old and afraid.

Bernhardt was lifting me and Bernhardt was holding me. Bernhardt lay atop me. It was time, I felt, to get in some practice soaring and gliding, so I leapt off the windowsill and rocketed away from the cars in the darkened parking lot, away and upward in the only direction available to me, straight toward white tiles and ceiling lights and that strange, artificial hanging garden made from tin pots and wooden spoons and heavy iron pans, all the things used to cook pancakes.

"What can I get you, sir?" called a girl's voice from below, and I looked down and saw our waitress, Rebecca, holding an order pad open in one hand and, in the other, a pencil poised to scribble. Did she think I was ready to put myself through another gruesome, paralyzing ordeal of choosing and ordering food? Rebecca stared up at me with that patient and slightly distant, more or less tolerant expression that waiters and waitresses everywhere use to defend against the subliminal, unexpressed appetites of finicky eaters—all the unassimilable longing, at table after table, for gentle sympathy and comfort. She waited. I hovered. Seen from high above, this girl became foreshortened in a way that made her look quite diminutive, younger and more childlike than in fact she actually was; and this weird visual effect and its corollary—Rebecca, the tall, black-haired high-school student, imagined as a toddler—made me think, as I drifted idly beside a small, upside-down omelette pan, of fairy-story scenarios featuring shrinking children and gigantic babies, ugly toads "kissed" into princes, and paupers crowned as kings, the whole inventory of enchantments and transformations that describe life in the realm of the unconscious.

"No food for me right this minute," I hollered at the tiny little creature standing beneath me.

"Coffee? Beer? A glass of milk?"

Milk sounded appealing. On the other hand, milk sounded not so good. "No thanks."

"Would you like to see a menu?" she called up to me, and I called back, "Later maybe. Now isn't the best time."

And because I had her alone, I said, "How would you like to come join the Young Women of Strength?"

Rebecca was looking directly up, and I could see her face and her hair spilling across her shoulders, the shapes of her breasts pushing against her Pancake House waitress costume.

"What's that?"

"It's a series of Wednesday-night alcohol-free socials at which girls aged fourteen to eighteen get together to talk about their plans for the future, without worrying about peer-group sexual pressures."

"Alcohol-free?"

"Yes."

"I can do that at home!" she exclaimed. Was she flirting? This was hard to imagine. Then again, it was not hard to imagine. In either case, I had the feeling that I might enjoy a chat with Rebecca. A chat with Rebecca could be just the thing. I asked her, "Do you have trained counselors running 'Leave It All Behind' workshops at home?"

"Leave what behind?"

"Anything you want, I guess. This and that, whatever's not working. It's up to you." Why couldn't I answer this perfectly sensible inquiry about my own outreach program?

"Like my mother and father who don't sleep in the same bed since my aunt Sylvia came to die of cancer in the spare room?"

"Exactly," I told her; and I noticed, then, that she was writing in her menu pad. Unfortunately, I was floating too far above her to make out characters or words.

"Can you tell me more about your program?" Rebecca asked me. She spoke with an interested though vaguely detached, clinical tone of voice, and I found myself feeling grateful for her company. I felt immediately at ease; it was relaxing to hang in the air and talk to Rebecca. I began by telling her, in the most general, cursory way, about my work and the work of others at the Institute. I then told her a little about the Krakower Institute itself, its history and philosophical position in relation to the various prominent psycho-analytic schools and traditions. This was an occasion to say a few words about Self / Other Friction Theory and its progenitor, Lawrence Mandelbaum, my analyst and former teacher, who, I recall, once took me aside and said, "Tom, in my experience, people meeting for the first time will disclose to one another most of the significant data of their lives, their dearest wishes and their worst fears, and sometimes, if you listen closely enough, their entire family legacies, usually within a minute and a half."

"Your teacher said that?"

"He did," I said. Then I felt myself drifting off course—

that is to say, I felt myself floating past Rebecca in a direction that would take me over the fish tank beside the cash register—so, straining hard against Bernhardt's warm hug, pushing with hands and arms against the Group counselor's mighty embrace, I reached out with one hand and grabbed hold of a pot lid suspended from a hook bolted into the ceiling.

"Do you believe that?" the girl asked me.

"What?"

"That people tell each other everything in the first few minutes." The way she watched me, her head slowly turning to follow me drifting gradually, steadily overhead, put me in mind of someone who has, by chance, looking up, noticed an intriguingly shaped cloud passing by, or maybe a kite let out on its string to a height at which it is on the verge of disappearing from view, a tiny, receding object whose distinct shape and brilliant coloring are no longer clearly discernible to the eye, only this black or pale yellow or reddish speck, a diamond or, possibly, one of those winged paper butterflies that weave and swoop across the sky, dragging serpentine tails tied from rags and ripped bedsheets.

"I believe in unlikely and unexpected affinities transacted between objects in a room," I called down to the pretty waitress. This was, I knew, a pretentious and fundamentally abstruse formulation, the worst kind of evasive, pseudo-academic psychology jargon; but what could I do?—I did not want to lose contact with Rebecca. I have to admit that I felt drawn to her. I clutched the pot lid tightly. The lid was my anchor.

"Objects?" she asked.

"People."

She agreed, "Yeah, I think I know what you mean. When I met Johnny Raab, I knew right away that we were, I don't know, similar. Johnny knew it too. We came from different backgrounds, but that didn't matter. Johnny's father was a doctor at the hospital—a real doctor." Here she paused. She made one of those "thoughtful" facial expressions people wear when they want you to know that they are considering their words. (I should say here that I have noticed, many times in my practice, that people having trouble expressing themselves really do furrow their brows—frequently!) Rebecca appeared, actually, embarrassed. Finally she spoke. "I'm sorry. That was rude. I shouldn't've said that about Dr. Raab being a real doctor."

"That's all right. Don't worry about my feelings. I'm comfortable with my professional credentials."

"I'm glad to hear that," she said.

Then she exclaimed, "Hey, here we are talking about life and everything, and I don't even know what I should call you!"

I have to confess that I took this as a blow. Hadn't she taken my order for blueberry pancakes? Hadn't she smiled at me across the room when I crawled like a baby across Bernhardt? Should I remind her that we had been introduced? Could she have forgotten? Would she recall Manuel's name, though not mine? Horrors.

Of course it was true that she was a worker in a family-style eating place. Her blue gingham dress gave her the appearance of a friendly milkmaid. People by the dozens introduce themselves to their waitresses in establishments like the Pancake House. Tired husbands, fathers of young children, chat them up.

"My name is Tom."

"Tom?" She sounded amazed, as if she did not believe me. This may have been due to a vestigial memory dating from our introduction by Manuel. He had called me Thomas, a minor variation but an important one. Rebecca, at some level, doubted my identity. Here was a crucial, possibly decisive juncture in our relationship.

"Or Thomas."

"Tom or Thomas? Which do you prefer?"

"Either. It doesn't matter. Pick one," I said. Things were getting interesting. What I mean to say is that I am not uninterested, in my professional life, in the business of naming, particularly nicknaming, which I regard as socially acceptable antisocial humiliation.

"What do your friends call you?"

"Friends?"

"Yeah. What do they call you?"

"Tom, I guess. Tom. Tom is fine. Just Tom, Tom," I repeated like a crazed, levitating obsessive.

"Okay, Tom. I'm Rebecca."

And what would happen if I told her that I already knew her Christian name? Might she conclude that I had somehow culled information about her private life? Would she think I was a stalker?

A simpler way of asking these questions might be, "Is there

any occasion more perilous, more absolutely life-threatening, than those first moments of meeting a new person?"

"You Rebecca, me Tom," I joked. Predictably, the old Tarzan routine fell flat, and I felt ridiculous for attempting it. How could I be so dumb? Was I made that nervous by Rebecca? I had diminished myself with a corny mode of discourse. Enough was enough. "What were you going to say about Dr. Raab, Rebecca?"

"Well, Tom, I liked Dr. Raab. He developed all these radical surgical techniques. He had a patent on a device that's used for making collapsed lungs stay attached to the insides of people's chests. Isn't that amazing? They always had cocktails at five o'clock on the dot at Johnny's house. It was pretty obvious that Mrs. Raab had a drinking problem. I mean, you could sit there and watch her face fall apart while she drank. It was like she became a different, older person. In English class we read *Dr. Jekyll and Mr. Hyde,* and I was convinced that it was about Mrs. Raab. She would pour a glass of bourbon to the top and walk around and never, ever spill. Then she'd lean back in her chair and her face would shatter. My mom and dad don't drink a drop. My mom's mom drank so much she died of liver disease. My mom and dad get mad at me if I drink even a little, even though I'm legal. I don't mind. It's because they love me. Do you like to drink? Never mind, that's none of my business. You don't look like a big drinker. Still, you can never tell about people. I think I want to become a doctor myself. Not a surgeon, though. With Johnny it was as if we'd known each other in the past. It was like we'd been waiting our whole lives to meet each other. We could practically answer each other's questions without asking any questions."

"Where is Johnny now?" I asked from over her head.

Her voice dropped, and she sounded, I thought, genuinely grief-stricken, at a loss, when she said, "Junior college." It was as if she had revealed to me, in saying this, that this boy had sickened and died. Is there anything more painful than the love felt by an adolescent?

She said, "I guess what Dr. Mandelbaum said is true, because I've just blurted every last little thing, haven't I?"

"I really don't know," I admitted to her. I was not sure it was a good idea to use a largely unprovable communication theory as the basis for a parlor amusement of the truth-or-dare variety.

Nonetheless I said, without knowing what I meant— without knowing what, if anything, I wished to provoke— "Feelings of mature love often take a long time to come to light, Rebecca."

And I thought, *Love?*

"Oh."

Was she crying? Were there tears? Or was this only an exciting illusion created by the tilted-back angle of her head? Here was a girl who showed a lot of throat. It is always so difficult to judge with certainty the sexual and courtship mannerisms of a younger generation.

"In fact," I explained to the girl, somewhat in the style of a lecturer in a classroom, "we mainly tell people things we don't know we're telling. Let's take my example. Here I am, as you can see, in Dr. Bernhardt's arms. Dr. Bernhardt is holding me in the air because he doesn't want me to throw cinnamon-raisin toast at Peter Konwicki. I don't really know *why* Dr. Bernhardt doesn't want me to throw any cinnamon-raisin toast at Peter Konwicki, who is basically a menace even if he is nice to children, but there it is. Dr. Bernhardt, or *Doctor* Bernhardt, I should say"—who, I ask, can resist clowning around about people's university degrees?—"*Doctor* Bernhardt saw me preparing to start a food fight, which is something I like to do at a dinner party. He therefore picked me up and started squeezing me, and as a result I've dropped the toast and flown out of my body, and now here I am in the air over everyone's heads, feeling sick to my stomach and hanging on to a pot lid!"

What point exactly was I trying to make? Something about the unconscious and its role in interpersonal communication? I was chattering on about other matters entirely. Was I making sense? Rebecca quickly jotted notes in her flipped-open menu pad. I found this comforting. Also comforting was her manner of occasionally looking up from writing, in order to make fleeting eye contact, then saying, quietly and without interrupting my train of thought, "Hmm," or "Yes, that's very interesting."

It was, I realized, a surprisingly dexterous portrayal of classical analytic attitude—surprising, in particular, from such a young person, and with no training in the field.

On the other hand, it was conceivable that Rebecca was merely taking a break to tabulate bills for her customers at tables and booths, only humoring me until she could politely excuse herself and disappear through the massive, swinging kitchen doors.

I could not, I felt, let this happen. It seemed to me that

everything, in that moment of hanging on to the pot lid and looking down at shouting and laughing analysts, at orange and pale white fish swimming in their glass tank adjacent to cash register and candy-bar display, at plates and glasses carried on trays held high by waitresses squeezing between blue tables and the chairs pushed back by people getting up, after eating, to order drinks, slap one another on the shoulder, and generally work the room—everything, by which I mean *something,* though I'm not sure what, depended on loving Rebecca and seeing her smile.

"Listen," I said to this girl standing on solid ground, "I've got to fly around up here for a while, and I'd be very happy if you'd join me."

"Me?"

"Why not?"

"I can't fly."

"Hey, look at me. Do I look like I know what I'm doing up here?" I said to her.

And I said, "Why don't you put away that pad and pencil and reach up here and take my hand?"

"Are you sure?"

"Yes."

"Really?"

"Absolutely."

"It's scary."

"I'll hold you," I told her, though I was not sure how I would do this while being restrained in Bernhardt's ferocious, amazing hug. Rebecca understood the problem. "How?" she asked.

"I'll hold your hand," was all I could offer.

"Promise?"

"Promise."

But it was clear that she was frightened and did not know what to make of things. "I've never done anything like this before," she said; and I suggested to her, in calming, professional therapist's tones—using to advantage, I hoped, the experienced interviewer's mild, upward inflection, more or less converting the statement to a question, a topic for careful contemplation, suggested less by word choice than by subtle modulations in pitch and volume at the close of the sentence—"All the more reason to try it out?"

Rebecca made an objection that would be difficult, if not impossible, to counter. "I work until eleven."

"What time is it now?"

"Don't you wear a watch?"

"I don't."

"I don't either."

"Hmm," I said.

She said, "The clock in the kitchen says it's a little before nine. But that clock's always fast."

I badly wanted her as a traveling companion. What could be sweeter than levitating through the roof alongside this mature young woman with the cascading hair?

"I'm due for a break at nine," she said. How nice it is, really, when a woman decides to, as they say, keep hope alive.

"Take a break now."

"I'll get in trouble."

"No you won't."

"Yes I will. You don't know what it's like around here, Tom. The managers watch every move you make. They know everything. They know if you drink a soda or eat a candy bar out of the cabinet. They know if you sneak out back for a cigarette. If you haven't changed the milk in the creamers, they know. They know how long you stay in the bathroom."

"I'll have you back on your feet in ten minutes," I said—a classic example of the male's willingness to make wild assurances to the female. In my favor was Rebecca's unhappiness in her job.

And I thought, *Please come flying.*

She gazed around the restaurant. She peered to her left and she peered to her right.

Please.

She considered.

Please, please.

She stared down at her shoes. She stared at them for a long time. Was she thinking about leaving the earth? Was she thinking about leaving everything behind?

Was she, in other words, a Krakower Institute Young Woman of Strength?

She folded closed the menu pad and tucked this, along with her pencil, into the roomy apron pocket stitched to the front of her blue dress. She looked up. She was answering my prayers. She swept back her hair, getting it out of her eyes, and she raised her hand to me. Her arm reached up across what seemed a great, almost insurmountable distance: I was in the sky and she was far below; and the visual impression, from such giddy heights, was of Rebecca's arm stretching beyond its normal or actual capacity, coming up toward me like something shooting straight from the ground, growing fast from its roots, up toward the clouds like the beanstalk in the children's tale. Here her arm came, white and beautiful.

There was her hand.

Quickly—I was afraid that if I hesitated she might lose heart and change her mind; or, even if she did not change her mind, we might reach too slowly for one another and, reaching too slowly, drift apart in midair, I veering out over the fish tank and across the room, she sailing away over the bar or into the kitchen or God knows where—quickly I let go of the hanging pot lid and, as best I could, waved my hand at Rebecca. Perhaps it is true that in those moments when we are about to touch, for the first time, another person, those moments while we wait to feel, against our own hand, the touch of another's with its strange fingers lightly brushing nails against our palm, so that the skin tingles not only on our hand but even in the most unexpected places, the small of the back or the slightly raised arch of a foot or the vulnerable, soft inside fold of a knee—perhaps in these moments when the routine comings and goings of life give way to some different condition, that condition of being on the verge of touching someone new, maybe at these times we feel more alive—*are* more inscrutably, unfathomably alive—than during any other. That was how I felt, tingling and breathless as I reached down to clasp Rebecca's hand in mine. She must have felt the same way or nearly the same way, because when our hands joined she shuddered and I heard her exclaim, "Ah, ah," as, inch by tiny inch, her heels lifted off the floor, then her toes, and she floated up to meet me.

"Hello," I said.

"Am I in the air? Am I really in the air?" she asked.

"You are."

"Is this flying?"

"It is."

"We're so high up. Lord, everyone is so small down there. Is this the ceiling? What happens if I bump my head? Can they see us from those little tables?"

"Sherwin can see us. And Peter Konwicki knows we're up here. He doesn't miss a thing."

"What about the man holding us? Will he mind my being up here? Won't he get tired?"

"Don't worry about Richard. He's very strong and determined. We have to trust him."

Holding Rebecca, my heart sped up and the world inside the restaurant slowed—everything *got* slowed down, or things as I saw them broke down, something like that. How to describe this? I could see, intensely and clearly, fish swimming in their tank beside the cash register. I saw the colors on the fish. Bernhardt gently shifted his grip around me, and my breaths became slower and steadier, slower and deeper; and I saw a shiny spoon dangling in the air beside Rebecca's head; and I saw, too, in great detail, as if photographically enlarged, rust in orange and brown blotches on the spoon. Light from above threw brightness across Rebecca, heat over the two of us. Peter Konwicki's voice rose loudly above others' in the noisy space: "He's unprofessional and shouldn't be allowed to have patients!"—followed with "Anybody can hang out a fucking shingle these days!" The air in the Pancake House was sweet with confectionery smells of food cooking. It was hard to say, in that first moment of Rebecca's ascension, what anything seen or heard had to do with any other thing, or with me, or with her.

At first things between us were awkward. It was like we had met in the sky for a blind date. We were holding hands and our movements together were the commonplace, embarrassed gestures made by people making guesses about one another's limits and desires. I tugged on her hand and she waved her arm, then pulled on me, and I floated over near her breast. I got my balance and frowned in a way intended to show her that I was not thinking about her breast. She kicked her feet; I tilted my body away. We were trying to avoid taking liberties. It was a dance of avoidance. You can see this kind of dynamic at work whenever a man teaches a woman with whom he is recently acquainted how to fish or shoot pool or throw a ball, and always the question is: "How much, and in what ways, can I feel her?"

Another way of asking the question might be: "What is this woman's body telling me, if her body is telling me anything at all, about her readiness to accept me as a lover?"

"Stop kicking," I told her.

"Sorry."

"You don't have to stick your arm out like that," I said.

"I don't?"

"Try this," I suggested, maneuvering her gradually closer, in order to gain leverage and twirl her, if I could and she would be willing, partway around, facing away from me.

"Mind the rusty spoon," I told her.

"I see it."

She settled back toward me and I got a faceful of her hair. Wasn't this what I had wanted all along? Rebecca's hair's smell was wonderful but difficult to classify—spicy in some way, and, for want of a better word, smoky, the perfume of wood burning in fireplaces.

"Do you build fires at home?" I asked her.

"Why do you ask?"

"Your hair. It smells like woodsmoke." I took a deep breath. The scent of Rebecca's black hair was an antidote to Richard's cologne and sweaty clothes and his breath in my face.

"We have a fireplace, but we don't use it. Probably everything in our house smells like soot, because the house is so old and moldy and rotten and gross."

She kicked a couple of times, and I gave her hand a squeeze, then said, "You don't smell like soot to me."

"Thanks," laughing.

I felt good. I felt happy and relaxed with my new friend. I said to her, "I know what you mean about smells in old houses. I love the eighteenth-century buildings along the riverfront."

"Is that where you live?" she asked me. Little by little, we were getting to know one another.

"No. South side on the other end of College Hill, in a house that looks like a tugboat. Past the first light after the old municipal swimming pool. How about you?"

"We live on the north side."

"Near the book factory?"

"I can see it from my window. That's where my dad works. He fixes the machines."

"How about that," I said; and she came right out, as the young will, and asked me, "Do you have children?"

"No."

"Why not?"

"No reason," lying.

"Does your wife want to have a baby?" I could feel her hand's pressure against mine, Rebecca's fingers holding my fingers and touching, on my ring finger, the gold band.

"We talk about babies." I felt, saying this, as if I were making a wrongheaded, compromising admission. Was I giving away information that properly belonged to Jane? Or was I merely regretting this necessary honesty, these polite formalities disguised as intimate disclosures—or was it the other way around, provocative intimacies hidden inside good manners?—in my conversation with Rebecca? Talking to the girl, holding her aloft while she kicked, I felt unfaithful. But to whom?

Rebecca? (Inevitably.)

Jane? (Unhappily.)

Maria? (Hardly, though, in a way, constantly.)

"Boy or girl?" Rebecca asked me. For a moment I was not certain what she was talking about. I was busy regretting my habit of wishing that I might become, briefly and at will, a different, more honorable person. Then I remembered. Children.

"Boy or girl, it doesn't matter," I told the flying waitress. It was my second lie in only a minute or two.

Rebecca confided, "I don't want children. Women are supposed to want children. Maybe when I'm older I'll want children. Johnny used to always talk about having them with me. After he left for college, he'd call on the phone, in the middle of the night, and start dreaming about the babies we were going to have. Sometimes we'd have a boy and a girl, sometimes a couple of each, and if Johnny had been out drinking then it would be a great big bunch of boys, a baseball team's worth of boys. It was like he was talking to himself. There I am, one room away from Aunt Sylvia dying from her cancer. It's the middle of the night and all I want to do is fall asleep and get out of school one day and move far away. Then the phone would ring and it would be Johnny, saying"—here Rebecca lowered her voice and spoke from the throat, imitating a teenaged boy's deliberately gruff, mock-authoritative delivery, a girl's imitation of a boy imitating a man—" 'I was just thinking about the two of us having our boys.' He thought he was being romantic. He thought I should love him for saying those things. How was I supposed to think about the rest of my stupid life? I regret not sleeping with him. He was my boyfriend, it wasn't like I was going to be *forced* to get pregnant. If you want to avoid getting pregnant, you can do that easily. I never relaxed. I was always saying no, no, no. I thought sex had to be a big deal. And it is! It *is* a big deal. I want it to be fun. What did I know at two in the morning when the phone rang and everybody else in the house was asleep or dying? I was mean. Do you think there's something bad going on with me?"

"Not really."

"You're wrong. I'm not normal. I spend all my time being scared. I don't like people my own age, but I don't want to get old either. Sometimes I think I'll be stuck working in this crappy joint for the rest of my life. By the way, you really shouldn't eat here. They use rancid milk in the pancake batter and the maple syrup is nothing but corn syrup with flavoring, and there's no real butter, and the cook never takes a bath or washes his hair, and there are roaches living in the oven, and the other day I saw a mouse."

"Wait a minute. Roaches live in the oven?"

"Yes."

"Don't they get cooked?"

"Of course they do. They're in there baking right now. But there are so many roaches in that oven. New ones keep moving in, and the burnt ones fall in the food."

"I'm sorry to hear that." I held Rebecca's hand tightly. I could not tell whether Bernhardt had been eavesdropping on our conversation. He continued to breathe against my neck. Rebecca said, "You seem like a nice man. There's no reason for you to eat bugs."

"Thank you."

"I mean it," she said; and I could tell, from the way she nuzzled against me, her body in its gingham dress curving softly at the hips as she bobbed up and down in the air, I could tell that she did.

Then Rebecca looked down and her eyes got wide. Her body tensed—I could feel this through her hand in mine—and her face got that expression people's faces get when something alarming comes into consciousness. Her tongue came out, once, then again; and her mouth stayed open, and she cried, "Oh, my God, we're so high! I don't like it up here! Will you put me down? People are staring at us. I want to get down!"

"Don't look at the ground."

"I'm dizzy."

"Look up."

"I'm scared."

"Close your eyes and breathe deeply," I said; and I could see, looking from table to table around the restaurant, that Rebecca was right: we were closely watched.

"I'm going to pass out! I'm passing out!" she cried. I squeezed her hand and shouted at her, "Pull yourself together! You're going to make me drop you! You'll make me drop you and Richard will drop me, and then where will any of us be?"

It was a question worth considering. It was unlikely that Rebecca or I, if released and dropped—Rebecca falling away from me, I tumbling from Bernhardt's arms—would suffer much in the way of honest-to-God physical hurt. We were not in fact terribly far off the floor. At the same time—and here is an important point, I think—we were quite high off the floor. We held one another, we were bound together in dependency; and our flying, this sensation of rising and hovering, was more than an imaginary event, neither dream nor fantasy. It was a complex and convincing ordeal that we created and shared and believed in—Rebecca and Richard and I, along with the analysts watching from their tables—together. You might say that our flying was the sensory and perceptual equivalent of a so-called psychosomatic illness. It is incorrect to say that the psychosomatically ill person fantasizes symptoms. Symptoms and illnesses manifesting psychosomatically—as the physiological "consequences" of obscure or extreme emotional turmoil—are no less real, no less medically verifiable, than, say, a cold or the flu caused by routine viral or bacterial contagion and infection. The true hypochondriac inhabits his condition, feels every ache and every fever. Rebecca and I, held up by Bernhardt, felt every dip and rise, every swift descent over the heads of our sitting and walking friends. Falling from the sky would be a shattering, bitter end to the affair.

"Don't let go of us," I pleaded to the man holding me. By then I think I realized that he had no intention of releasing me, that there was, for Richard as well as for me, something significant—something movingly, vividly pornographic—taking place.

"I love you, Tom," he whispered; and his arms in red sleeves closed tightly around me, reaching around my arms and across the lower part of my chest; and also his hands, Richard's open, enormous hands reached down from my chest to cover the soft area over my stomach, and I felt Richard's fingers extending around either side of me, pressing into my ribs.

I could feel, more and more as the night went on, the overwhelming weight of him, Richard's whole body pushing against me and squashing me. I was feeling sore all over from the heaviness of Bernhardt crushing me, and it was hard to get air.

"Close your eyes," I said to Rebecca, who thrashed and struggled like a person drowning.

"I'm going to be sick!" cried the girl.

"You'll be all right," I assured her, in spite of the fact that I was feeling queasy myself—as I had been all night since taking off, propelled by Bernhardt on my own flight. Rebecca's hand in mine felt cold and wet with her sweat. We were both sweating. There was moisture on her face and her arms. I was afraid her hand would slip out of mine.

"Going to be sick," she said again. Her voice trembled and her long hair fell forward across her face, sticking there. Her face was sallow white. She was clearly wretched. I pulled on her hand and swung her a little distance through the air, bringing her close to a Dutch oven hanging from a thin metal wire attached to the ceiling.

"Throw up into the pot," I told her, and she leaned her head into the Dutch oven and vomited.

"Good girl, that's a good girl," I said while Rebecca heaved and spat. I was trying to calm her. It is embarrassing to throw up in public, and no one who does this wants to feel reprimanded.

Her head hung halfway inside the pot, and her hair draped around its rim, encircling the black outside of the Dutch oven. She reached up with her free hand, gathered the hair into a ponytail, and held it away from the iron cauldron and her neck. Her neck above the blue dress was bare. Rebecca held her hair in her hand, and I saw, on the back of her neck, across the spine and beneath Rebecca's hairline, the tiny, recognizable pattern of freckles and moles.

It was a detail from Jan Brueghel the Elder's *A Woodland Road with Travelers,* one of Brueghel's small and intimate, perspectival paintings of Dutch peasants in a landscape. *A Woodland Road with Travelers* shows men and women with their children on a journey, carrying burdens and leading hobbled and swaybacked draft animals that draw broken-down carts piled and overspilling with household belongings and more people, the cart's drivers and, presumably, the very old who cannot walk over the stones and brambles and fallen leaves and the tree roots that stick out everywhere from the forest floor—a caravan of the poor making their way inexorably along a road that never was a road, underneath old trees that bend down over the heads of the people, blotting out the sun. Deep blue sky, three or four dark birds, the forest's edge, and one or two painted clouds are apparent in the immediate distance. In the lower left foreground, beneath a tree, lies the bleached, intact skeleton of a fallen horse. The animal's skull is huge and, as is true of everything in Brueghel's work, observantly painted. Two finely dressed men—aristocrats? royal messengers? prosperous thieves?—ride on horses past the skeleton, through the trees and into the woods. Do they notice the bones of the fallen animal? Is a dead horse cause for concern? Where are the men going? What danger are they riding toward? The pilgrims with their overloaded carts, on the other hand, mainly travel away from the viewer; and there is a feeling that these good people have left their homes and whatever blood ties exist for them. They plod with their loads toward the break in the forest, toward a town or village with its church steeple faintly discernible, rising up at the vanishing point on the horizon. A few travelers, and a small black, brown, and white dog have stopped to sit and rest beneath the trees in the lower right corner of the scene. The dog peers back along the road, back into the dark woods toward unseen things that have been abandoned or lost in the recent past;

and the dog gazes, as well, into the eye of the viewer standing before the painting. Caravans proceed toward and away from the town. The wealthy horsemen ride heedlessly into the forest. The mood of the painting is neither happy nor sad, frightening nor liberating; it is all these things.

If you look at the painting, you will see the dog staring out at you. If you move to the left or the right, the dog's eyes will find you—exactly as the eyes of figures in paintings are expected to do.

The dog connects the people in the painting to the world outside the painting. It is as if Brueghel's peasants have been cast out of the living world in order to wander through the painting.

It was Jan Brueghel the Elder's little dog, I was sure, glaring at me from the naked back of Rebecca's neck, when Rebecca leaned over to throw up in the open Dutch oven hanging from its strong, thin cable screwed into the Pancake House & Bar ceiling.

What could it mean to be gazed at by a lonely dog inscribed on the neck of a girl vomiting in midair? There was no way of knowing, though I suspect this manifestation of the dog provided a clue about my role as a transitional figure in Rebecca's life.

It is important in my profession to study these kinds of signs, not as portents heralding so-called real or impending phenomena, but as indicators of unspoken predilections and attractions on the part of the beholder. Readers of symbols are forever at the mercy of desire. I saw an art-historical dog on Rebecca's neck because I imagined Rebecca herself looking inarticulately, longingly backward, searching through meta-phoric dark forests—for a man like me.

She let her hair fall from her hand. She drooled into the black pot. I held her other hand. Rebecca's left hand was hanging in the air and her right hand was holding my left hand. Our hands were locked together. We were like a pair of worried, unpracticed dance partners. My arms were held in place by Bernhardt's arms. Rebecca's hair fell across her back and the dog withdrew from sight. Bernhardt lifted me in his hug. He was my father. I was able to learn from his good example, and to say, calmly, to Rebecca:

"I'm here."

"Fuck," she said.

She raised her head and brought up her arm and mopped, with her dress's long, blue cotton sleeve, her face.

"Do you feel better?" I asked.

"Uhf," she said.

"Can you try flying?"

"I don't know."

In no sense did Rebecca's episode of vomiting make her less attractive to me; on the contrary, she became more beautiful and sympathetic as a character in my life.

I watched her spit.

"You have some on your chin."

"Where?"

"There."

Obviously, I was unable to raise my hand to her face. I wished I could have wiped her off. It would've been a brave, intimate gesture. I nodded my head and shifted my eyes.

"Lower," I said.

She scrubbed with her open hand. With her other hand she held tightly to my hand. Was separation as frightening to Rebecca as it was to me? Was she apprehensive of solitude?

"A little lower."

"Lower?"

"You've got it," I said.

Her eyes were watery and circumscribed with black shadows. Rebecca's lips were red.

"You're beautiful," I told her.

"I'm sick."

"We'll take things slowly," I promised.

And we did. I gave Rebecca plenty of time to catch her breath, to clean up or at least pat her hair into place and wipe her mouth, that sort of thing, and then we began, hand in hand, a clockwise circuit of the room. Along the way I pointed out people below, telling Rebecca their names and embellishing their stories with friendly Institute gossip, occasionally waving and smiling if the person under scrutiny happened to look up and spy us gliding through the air above everyone's heads.

"That's Elizabeth Cole. She's in her third marriage, to a man named Deavers who is at least half a foot shorter than she is and teaches biology at the high school. The man on her right is Mike Breuer. Mike is a former Episcopal minister. Before that he was a star running back for the Kernberg College Colonels. Now he's a fine therapist."

Mike saw us and smiled—as if he knew I was speaking well of him—and Rebecca whispered in my ear, "He seems like a nice man."

"Mike is nice," I agreed. And why not? The man is, I would say, extraordinarily friendly and companionable for an ego psychologist—it's his Protestantism leaching through the analytic attitude, in the form of a seductive, earnest affability. People always wish to confide in Mike, because they identify him as trustworthy.

"Who's the guy dressed like Abraham Lincoln?" Rebecca asked me. She was pointing.

"That's Sherwin Lang."

"Oh."

"Sherwin is one of my favorite people," I said.

"How come?" asked Rebecca. We were, at this point, directly above Lang's table; and I could see, looking straight down, that Sherwin and Mike had well-defined bald spots. Sherwin, as I may have mentioned, wore his hair long and brushed back from his forehead. I saw now that this was a ruse. No amount of styling and combing will ever conceal significant hair loss. Lang's skull was surprisingly apparent from above; and the similarity—in shape, circumference, and approximate position—between his and Mike's baldness patterns was, I thought, striking, particularly considering the different techniques each man adopted in relation to his bald spot, and what these techniques revealed about the men in relation to one another. Mike, wearing his hair crew-cut short, appeared from overhead to be the more honest and forthright fellow—a man without evident disguises. Lang's hair was deliberately forged into a kind of mane, combed into those high black-and-gray swells that seemed poised to crash over and swamp his white and unprotected grotto of naked head.

"Sherwin's an interesting person," I said to Rebecca as,

together, we peered down at the drinker and the former semi-narian. These two men, buddies over many years, functioned socially as complements to one another, and were therefore, in my opinion, good examples of what I like to call compatible incompatibles. How often do we see this in friends and married couples? It's the story of Jack Sprat and his wife, that old rhyme about the economies of attracted opposites. But the fat wife / skinny husband situation also hints at the ways in which manifestly dissimilar individuals recognize in one another the most basic, hidden affinities. When we love a person who is strange to us, it is not as a rule mere strangeness that brings us into deeper affection; on the contrary, we feel moved by what is shared and historical: a certain kind of good or bad home, perhaps, the childhood full of love or the childhood without friends, a lonely mother or the father who drinks, the craving for solitude and a terror of solitude, all the exciting and providential things that make the groundwork for what we call, for lack of a better name, personality.

Was it possible that Mike Breuer, this sober father of three, with his clear blue eyes and toothy smile, found in Sherwin Lang a cathartic, operatic expression of his own dilemmas, fantasies, and fears?

And, for his part, did Sherwin "use" Mike to feel more at home in the world?

And where did I fit in? How did my career as a balding man correspond to Sherwin's, to Mike's? Peter Konwicki, one table over from Sherwin, showed baldness of a comparatively different sort—sweeping and absolute, as if the treacherous workings of Konwicki's mind obviated the need for hair in any style or amount. I cautioned Rebecca, "That man over there wants to destroy me. He claims to like children, but he's a fiend."

Rebecca squeezed my hand. It felt to me that we were growing closer up here in the air, and so naturally I wondered if it would be appropriate for me to warn her, as well, about myself.

"Uh, listen," I began; then blathered, somewhat maniacally, at the waitress, "I'm confused. I don't know what I want. Do you understand what I mean? How could you? You're young and you have life ahead of you. I act like a baby in public. I spit water at my colleagues. I prop trash cans against their doors so that the trash will spill into their offices, then I knock and run down the hallway. I think it'll make me happy to play these tricks, and people will laugh, but no one ever appreciates my jokes, and I wind up depressed. Later I break down in tears during important meetings. My marriage is in trouble. The problem is that I don't know how to be a man. I'm the right *age* to be a man, but does that make me a man? Jane puts up with my ridiculous theories about—about— everything under the sun! Why am I so afraid of children? Why can't I talk to Jane about a child? Is it because I want to *be* the child? I want to be the child! I want to be the child! Why do I think I can help people? Children can't help people! Children are the ones who need help!"

What had brought this on? Why was I having this interview with myself, blurting these embarrassing things? Quickly, I tried to achieve a little composure. "I only thought, Rebecca, that if you're going to fly with me, if you're going to be up here where everyone below can see up your dress, and not down there clearing tables and collecting tips, I thought you should know what sort of person I am."

Rebecca looked straight at me and said—I liked her for this, though was uncertain how to take it, exactly—"I figured you were royally screwed up when you couldn't decide between pancakes or eggs for dinner. Pancakes or eggs? What's the big deal? You looked like you were about to have a nervous breakdown. It was funny."

"Funny?"

"Yeah."

"It wasn't funny when it was happening," I told her, sadly, and felt, as I almost always do, misunderstood. But she said—incredibly, I thought, for a high-school student—"I know you were in pain. But other people's pain is funny, don't you think?"

I knew, then, that I was going to fall for this girl. I could feel it coming on. I gazed at her face beside mine. Everything about Rebecca seemed right to me. I had an urge to laugh. What is more enjoyable than a brand-new infatuation? I felt uncomfortable in a thoroughly pleasant way. Were my hand and fingers damp against hers? Could she feel my nervousness? Rebecca's eyebrows were dark. Did she pluck them? What did girls do, these days, in the way of erotic grooming? Her cheeks and the bridge of her nose showed freckles sprayed across the skin. Eyes were brown but appeared black in her freckled, damp face.

I asked her, "Are you feeling better? Is your stomach settled? Do you want to glide down to the kitchen and get a ginger ale?"

"I'm okay. I'm used to throwing up. I do it all the time at home. You'll probably advise me to see a psychiatrist."

"I would never tell anyone to see a psychiatrist. Psychiatrists are medical doctors. They emphasize diagnostics and pharmacology. I'd tell you to talk to that man in the flannel shirt."

"The fat guy smoking a cigarette?"

"Dan Graham specializes in eating disorders and substance abuse problems."

We were over the fish tank, positioned at what aviators call twelve o'clock, headed like a pair of tangled-up Macy's Thanksgiving Day Parade balloons past the cash-register counter, out across the open, middle part of the restaurant, toward windows overlooking town and, rising above town and the river, College Hill. Richard Bernhardt was our mooring. Fog had thickened and city lights were indistinct. Every now and again thunder rumbled. Rain from the north was taking its time getting here. There was no horizon line visible outside the windows, only fogginess and, permeating the night, a radiant, atmospheric glow, the city in the mist. The hospital roof alone was visible on the skyline, a beacon in the outer dark.

Indoors, down below Rebecca and me, Dan Graham exhaled smoke, then tipped cigarette ashes onto the floor. It was easy to see, from above, how huge and round the man was. Smoke from his cigarette drifted up, pooling beneath the ceiling. I got a whiff of the smoke, and for some reason that had nothing to do with unwholesome aspects of the habit, this smell of cigarette made me sad for Dan. He appeared, as smokers do, with their puffing and dragging, their attention to the rituals of striking the match and applying the flame and so on, quite alone—an obese, preoccupied man without a friend in the world. And it was true: no one was talking to Dan. To his left and his right were people who had pulled chairs close together; and there were, at Dan's table, three empty chairs left by analysts who, finished eating, had pushed their seats back, gotten up, and marched away in search of better tables with better, more healthy and outgoing people at them. The party was disintegrating into a collection of isolated small parties.

My idea of Dan's loneliness came mainly from watching what was taking place at the table behind Dan's back.

Leslie Constant, the Englishwoman, was gazing at Sherwin Lang. These two were, by this point in the evening, deep in their sexual negotiations, establishing, over bacon and eggs, toast, coffee, and beer, all the important sadomasochistic patterns and dynamics of the relationship ahead: who would come on strong, and who would express a characteristic ambivalence; who would regularly weep, and who would be perceived as the cause of all the tears; who would become doting and remorseful after a fight, and who would rely on casual sarcasm and renewed quarreling to mediate the terms of reconciliation and attachment. Everything—though who can ever really say how things will play out in other people's entanglements?—seemed contained in the archetypal tableau struck by this man and this woman with their dinner plates and Sherwin's impressive collection of empty brown beer bottles pushed aside so that nothing might stand between them. Leslie was the designated aggressor. Her elbows were propped on the table and her chin rested in her hands. Her blond head tilted sideways and downward, slightly—forcing Leslie to gaze up in order to make eye contact with Sherwin. She was looking at Lang in exactly the manner of a timorous girl trying out her charms on a handsome, withdrawn adult. Has this stock approach ever failed as a feminine court-ship tactic? Sherwin crossed his arms before his chest. He appeared, in his weird, too-tight coat, like a subject for a daguerreotype. Lang held on tightly to his bottle; he pressed himself against the rigid, wooden back of his chair—how else survive Leslie's intimate onslaught?—the seducing alcoholic in retreat, giving the woman permission to answer his seduc-tion, to push in closer and closer, and to signal, with her body craning toward his across their table, her woundedness, her availability, her readiness to collapse into dependency.

At the next table over, Peter Konwicki seemed to be leading a small, intense, by-invitation-only academic confer-ence; all his child-psychology trainees listed heavily toward their table's masculine center of power. Konwicki tipped his chair back, using it as a rocker. He crossed his legs. This was a strong move, because it made Peter look precariously unbalanced, yet—with one leg angled up and hoisted over the other, leaving only a single ugly brown shoe touching the floor—daringly in control of his situation. He rocked. The students leaned in. You could say, watching Peter tip farther and farther back in his Pancake House chair, that he was acting out his own inner condition, a state I would briefly describe as an *a priori* primary process imbalance, regulated by extraordinary superego functioning. This impression of deep psychic instability mirrored in physical disequilibrium was accentuated by Konwicki's hypermanic talking style: much waving of the arms and hands. He gestured at his followers like a man lecturing to the back rows in a large hall—or, more to the point, I thought, like someone on the street shouting complicated directions to foreigners.

"I want you all to observe closely and pay attention to what you see," he instructed the students. "We have a rare opportunity, tonight, to witness a man in the throes of what lay people call a nervous breakdown." At this point Konwicki leaned forward on his tilted-back chair. This allowed him to make quite dramatic rocking motions. He lowered his voice and spoke in loud stage whisper. "Direct your eyes to the torrentially sweating hands and arms and the rashy contact dermatitis around the neck. Notice also Tom's violently labored breathing and periodic twitching, and the convulsing of the hips, legs, and feet. These are symptoms of a catastrophic anxiety disorder that is manifestly sexual in nature. The subject has regressed to a classically pre-oedipal position, in order to reorganize psychosexual reality and survive trauma. The fixation on unassisted flight and the collapse of subjective time are diagnosable side effects and, while not common, also not unknown in the literature. Would anyone care to comment on the probable outcome?"

"Psychotic break with sudden onset of schizophrenic episodes, uh, possibly hostile behavior leading to a gradual dissolution of coherent identity, necessitating antipsychotic medicalization and . . . let's see . . . lifelong hospitalization?" guessed Konwicki's nervous star pupil, Bob.

"Complete reorientation of sexual identity and a basic repudiation of socially binding mores and conventions, including the marriage contract?" predicted a second-year candidate (female, brunet, named Katharine) specializing in gender assignment as a function of social class.

"Watch and learn," said Konwicki.

It was, it must've been, after nine at night. Wind blew against the northern windowpanes. The wind carried the clouds that drifted off the river. No one was eating anymore. A family that had been sharing a booth near the door was gone. I had not noticed them paying their bill. Their table was a mess and so was the floor around it; small children had been there. The two teenagers in a corner by the restrooms were, I saw, still nestled down in brooding, reclusive, adolescent communion. The boy put money in a miniature jukebox on the wall beside the table; then the girl and he leaned heads forward across the tabletop to study selections. He rotated the jukebox knob. They breathed into one another's faces. I imagined that this boy and girl were Rebecca's sexually experienced friends, waiting for her to punch out at eleven so they could all escape into the boy's car. Sexuality notwithstanding, the teenagers looked like children to me, which is to say they looked chubby and unformed, whereas Rebecca had become, in my eyes, a woman. I stared at her bone structure, the shadowy, depressed temples and thin nose and boyish, squared jawline; and I was afraid I might giggle with pleasure, and she would misunderstand my feelings and not be flattered. She smelled to me like woodsmoke and some kind of unfamiliar soap and—faintly, not at all unpleasantly—vomit. It was impossible to kiss her without everyone seeing. I could hear, as we sailed beneath the foam-tile ceiling, fragments of conversation, little comments people made about therapy, about Krakower Institute business, about each other and about the two of us, me and Rebecca transported off the ground in Bernhardt's arms.

It was the commentary from my own booth that I found most interesting and threatening.

"Look at them up there, Manuel. This can't be a good thing. Tom should act his age and be more professional. He should know better. He only wants to eat her pussy," said Maria.

Manuel replied, "What has Tom done? He has reached out his hand in friendship to a young person. Perhaps it is true that our friend enjoys a fantasy of passionate cunnilingus with a beautiful girl. Men in cafes are known to dream of the waitress."

"This place is a far cry from a cafe, Manuel. And that girl is a teenager. She's in high school." Maria sounded angry and mean; she cried out, loudly enough for everyone, including Rebecca, to hear, "Tom is going too far! He's going too far!"

Manuel answered—brilliantly, I thought—"Tom is a man."

"I think it's sick." Maria went on, "The whole older man–younger woman thing gives me the creeps. Tom may be a man, but he's also married to a wonderful woman."

"He must create his own choices in life. Maria, you know this. You counsel people in their, how do you say, relationships. We must not tell Tom how to be a man."

"The girl will be the one who gets hurt, Manuel. She'll have to live with this after Tom has forgotten all about her."

"I don't know. I think that maybe you are, I think the word is 'generalizing,' " said Manuel. This was, of course, a vague and ineffectual rebuttal, and therefore a possible concession to Maria's vision of psychosexual reality. She sensed the European's uncertainty about ordinary domestic interpretations of the power structures in love. She played her trump card.

"What would Jane think?"

"That is none of our business."

"I might just make it my business," said Maria.

Hearing this, I had a real desire to vacate the premises, as they say. Maria, it seemed plain, was enraged over my seduction of Rebecca, a woman half Maria's age. But was that all there was to it? Was Maria also distressed over Rebecca's seduction—expressed symbolically as flying, vomiting into the iron pot, showing me the little dog, and so forth—Rebecca's seduction of me? Was Maria declaring a vestigial attachment, an expectable reluctance to watch her former lover function erotically in a context that excluded her? Did I, in other words, have a chance, someday soon, of sneaking with Maria down the windowless, creaking stairwell, through the cellar and past the old boiler, into the Krakower Institute book and manuscript vault?

There was no way to find out. Talking sweetly to Maria would cause Bernhardt to crush my ribs.

It was, I felt, under the circumstances, best to remain safely above things, to keep Rebecca close, and travel, if we could and her stomach might allow this and her boss would not fire her, up through the ceiling and into the sky, out of the pancake restaurant and away beneath the stars, over the misty city with its river coursing through and its hospital roof shining above everything like a pharaoh's grave.

How far could we go? How high? I gave Rebecca's hand a tug, and her body obeyed. She rested against me. We were snuggling. I could smell the vomit on her breath, faintly, and her black hair's fireplace scent; and I could smell Bernhardt, of course, his clothes and cologne and his breath; and the bitter cigarette exhaust clouding the room above Dan Graham. Ceiling lights in smoky air looked yellow and greasy; and the lights gave off a perfume of their own—the sugary funk of electrical wiring cooking its rubber insulation. I smelled coffee and something acrid baking in the kitchen. Roaches? I had Bernhardt behind me and Rebecca in front of me. We were all pressed together. Rebecca was tall and long. She was a good fit. I did not, I realized at that moment, know her last name. I made a mental note to ask her later. Her hair was fantastically thick, and I could not see through it to Brueghel's dog.

Bernhardt's arms were untiring. I admired the man. Admiration was not something I'd ever felt for Richard. I said to him, "Richard, your panama hat is digging into the back of my head."

"Sorry, Tom."

"It's all right. If you angle your head. A little."

"Is that any better?"

"Well . . ."

"How about if I go this way?"

"That's good. Much better. Are you comfortable with your neck twisted that way?"

"No problem, Tom."

"Great."

"I'm not squeezing too hard, am I?" Bernhardt asked me. I frankly thought Richard was squeezing a bit assertively, but as he had been considerate enough to inquire regarding this matter, I felt I should mind my manners and answer, politely:

"No."

"You're sure, Tom?"

"I'm positive. It's nice."

"You feel secure?"

I took a raspy breath. "Pretty much."

"Because in my opinion, Tom, that's the most important thing there is in life. A feeling of security."

"I agree, Richard"—wheezing.

"You speak up and let me know if there's anything I can do that will make you cozy," offered Bernhardt in his low, low voice; and once again I felt the thing that must have been, I was certain of this, the man's erection against my back.

Yes. There it was. There was no getting away from it.

On the other hand, was it truly, actually Bernhardt's erection? Given that Bernhardt was holding me in a bear hug, and that Bernhardt's stomach and the fronts of his legs were utterly mashed into my back and the backs of my legs, it was also and therefore the case that I was—in bodily, purely "physical" terms—at least half a foot higher off the ground than he.

I might have felt Richard's boner against my *leg,* but not, probably, against my back. I could be mistaken, though.

Rebecca turned her head and said, over my shoulder, to

Bernhardt, "Hi, we haven't really met. I'm Rebecca. I was your waitress."

How rude of me to have forgotten introductions. And how stupid. It was too late, now, to control their meeting, and to keep Bernhardt's contact with Rebecca at a minimum.

Bernhardt said, "I remember you. You had a wonderful way of helping Tom here get through a tough decision about his dinner. Not many people can show such calm in a crisis. That's a real talent you have. You might think about a career in psychology."

"Really?" asked Rebecca.

"I wouldn't lie to you," said the big man to the young girl with the dog on her neck. This got me mad. Why couldn't I have been the one to say nice things about Rebecca's prospects? .

I countered Bernhardt. "Don't rush into a profession, Rebecca. It's important to experiment and find work that's right for you. What you want to do is go to a decent liberal arts school and take a variety of courses in different fields. Enjoy yourself, read a few good books, play some intramural sports, and see what interests you."

She said—and made the idea sound absolutely depressing—"My mom wants me to go to Kernberg."

"Hmm," I said.

Bernhardt practically shouted, "Kill 'em, Colonels!" Then he quieted down and said, "The place has changed since I went. There's the brand-new veterinary school. Coed dorms."

Was this supposed to be incentive? It was not at all surprising to hear Manuel, seated and drinking coffee with

Maria at the vinyl-and-Formica booth immediately behind Richard—it was not surprising to hear the Kleinian pipe up and exclaim (to the extent that this man ever *exclaimed* anything), "Resist the mother! Taste the forbidden pleasures in life!"

"You're such a prick, Manuel," said Maria. "Why don't you just invite her to lie down here on the table so you can have your way with her on top of our plates?" Maria peered up at Rebecca and said, "Listen, honey, don't pay any mind to these creeps. They see you as a sexual object. They're threatened by your vitality."

What could be said about this? Maria was right, up to a point; and it was inevitable, I suppose, that she would create a job for herself as Rebecca's alternative, "good" mother.

Maria gave the girl some advice about sex and power. In doing so, she sounded an unwittingly contradictory and revealingly carnal note, ironically undermining her cherished position as a mature, financially independent woman who can take or leave men.

"Fuck 'em," she told Rebecca.

It might be useful, at this juncture, to pause and study, for a moment, the developing interpersonal situation: the weary old allegiances in decline, the new erotic configurations taking precedence; the relational matrix in flux around the question of a young waitress's college plans. As every educated person these days knows, our criticisms and judgments of others' lives are at least occasionally meaningful—in the opinion of some workers in my field, almost always so—as covert communications about our own attitudes, dispositions, and needs.

However, some of what we say about *ourselves* when we babble sentimentally or resentfully about family and friends (or about institutions like the Krakower Institute, or even made-up characters populating a story) expresses more than the solitary Self in action; rather, offhand commentary and gossip about others reveals insights and perceptions that are unarguably public and universal, common to humanity.

This is another way of saying that the things we believe about parents and lovers are, more often than not, true.

It is my hope to make a picture of things *as they were,* that April night at the Pancake House & Bar, and, through this process, faithfully reveal my own character and the characters of my companions, in this way say something worthwhile about what I call the verifiability in emotional experience.

Rebecca was with me in the air. She was in the air because she had taken my hand in hers. She was a Young Woman of Strength, and I wanted her beside me. Richard anchored me in place. Richard was in love with Maria; he had shown this by choking on a piece of her sausage. Maria, a marriage counselor, had never married. Richard wrapped his arms around me. Richard's arms were my reason for flight. Flying after eating breakfast food made me feel sick, though staring at a fixed point while buzzing around beneath the ceiling helped settle my stomach. The top of the hospital was one such fixed point, Sherwin Lang's bald spot another. Sherwin was not making any big movements. Leslie was encroaching on him, and he was, in effect, playing dead. Mike watched these two as, in movement and stillness, their gestures and poses, each told the other what would and would not be permissible in bed.

Mike's smile hid rage and envy. Elizabeth looked at Mike, and she pulled back her hair, showing Mike her ears. When two people in a group pair off, others around begin pursuing mates. Elizabeth wanted Mike. Manuel wanted Jane. The teenagers in their corner wanted each other. Bernhardt wanted Maria, and I wanted Maria, and Maria wanted Bernhardt, and I had him; I was his child. Maria was beyond my reach, and so, as an adaptive protection against Sherwin and Leslie—a way not to feel unchosen and lonely in this room where, everywhere you looked, erotic love was, as we like to say in the business, "in process"—in order not to feel too melancholy and afraid, and in order to create, if I could, a sense of balance and proportion in my life, I had selected Rebecca for my female partner. I risked disapproval from my colleagues. Then again, discretion is an equivalency of professionalism in the psychoanalytic community. Bernhardt's erection pressed hard against my back. The teenagers playing their jukebox almost kissed, as Konwicki kept from crashing backward in his chair. The world outside the windows was abruptly illuminated by distant lightning. I saw the cars and trees, and then these things were gone. Thunder followed. Maria spoke in a low voice to Manuel. Manuel understood that my embrace of Rebecca was a signal to him that I recognized and accepted his affection for Jane. Soon he would use tiredness and a busy day tomorrow as excuses to finish his coffee, say goodbye, and go home.

But he would not go home.

He would drive to my house with its front door painted red and the little windows upstairs painted shut.

It was not hard to imagine Manuel parking and getting out of the car, easing the car's door closed. The Pritchetts' television is always audible in the evenings from their house next door. This night—as I knew it to be, and as I *imagined* it to be—this night, the stars are obscured by fog that colors the sky white, almost, with light from the city. Jane's tulips border the driveway on both sides. Pale yellow, bright pink, red. They have begun to bloom. It is likely that Manuel—whose personality pretty much conforms to stereotypically American expectations regarding the characterological traits of southern-European intellectuals, meaning that his is a personality, or persona, that could aptly be described as an amalgam of subtle, implied aesthetic sensibilities—it is likely that Manuel will take time to appreciate the tulips; he'll pause and bend over, at some point during his stroll up the drive to the red front door, not to sniff a yellow or a red flower, because that might seem vulgar; rather, to engage in a swift and confident physical gesture acknowledging beauty, a kind of semiotic rehearsal for the much more cunning gestures and motions required, once he's inside my house, to put Jane at ease and make her receptive. A shrug here, a nod or small movement of the head or hand there. It's very easy when you know what you're doing. Manuel bends over and prepares himself for my wife; he gets his nose close to her garden, even though there is no one around to witness him doing this. And Jane will not be surprised when she sees Manuel standing on our porch in the night, not really. She might pretend to be surprised—and she is! Jane is, in that moment of pretending, genuinely flustered, disoriented in the most pleasurable way—but mainly Jane is satisfied and happy, a condition she masks by acting fidgety, uncertain. Would he like a drink? Oh, please come inside. Jane has to reach awkwardly around Escobar to latch the door and, in this confusion in which they almost touch, he refuses the drink. Then he reconsiders, because she is imploring him. Are you sure? What can I get you? She wants a drink. They are in the living room. They don't have much time. What's faster? Do you have the . damned drink or turn it down and possibly get hung up in a snag over formalities, the proper way to function as guest and hostess? Manuel has the opportunity at this point to try out an uncharacteristically goofy joke. The joke is that Tom has been "held up" at the Pancake House. It doesn't matter that this is neither funny nor recognizable to Jane as a witticism. In a way, that's the point. It's Manuel's first cruelty. He has the drink with Jane, because he feels slightly guilty about his wisecrack. Already he has begun denying her access to his thoughts and feelings. It would be terrible if she knew he had a sense of humor. Things can proceed with dignity only if all the polite steps are taken. And that's exactly right. Drinking the drink is the correct thing to do.

But no.

Manuel was not yet getting up to begin the long drive north through the city's broken-down districts. He was *not* on his way to lower the straps of Jane's backless dress from her shoulders.

He was sitting in the bright orange booth by the partly curtained window at the Pancake House & Bar. The window beside the booth looked out on the hospital roof. Maria was speaking to Manuel, and he was nodding his head in accompaniment to her whispering. The hospital's roof was immense, a lit-up temple that dominated everything in the night. I stared through the restaurant window, through the damp glass and the thickening fog, out at the illuminated pyramid; and it appeared, this structure, as I watched it hovering above our city lost in mist—it appeared to grow a tiny bit in size. What kind of hallucination was this? The roof looked, more accurately, as if it might be coming closer, a detached structure slowly approaching from the direction of the river district. Was it, in fact, a spaceship? Other city buildings had disappeared inside clouds that seemed to come down to ground level. Even the Kernberg College music building, the former academy for orphans that adorns the top of the hill, this fine old nineteenth-century building with its turrets and domes and stained-glass windows, the L-shaped wings leading to other wings beneath copper roofs stained green over the years—even the red-brick orphanage was invisible in the fog. Or was it? Was that it, off in the far distance? It was impossible to say. Shapes and lights appeared, then went away, then manifested again. The entire downtown was effectively gone, a ghost town. Here came the golden pyramid. How impressive this was. Could it have been—was it at all possible?—that the hospital roof's approach was an illusion caused by atmospheric moisture and reflected light? Did anyone else, happening to put down a fork or knife or cup and gaze momentarily out a northern window, notice that the top of the new municipal health-care tower—the intensive care unit, the maternity ward, and the private suites, to be exact—was sneaking up on us?

Richard's breath blew against my neck. From the other side of my face came Rebecca's. There was no air for me to breathe except exhalations from these two people. The moles covering Jane's back will never, I thought while hanging aloft in Bernhardt's grasp, seem to Escobar like a Winslow Homer or a Bierstadt painting of the grandiose, thrilling American West. Granted, this estimation of Manuel's imaginative limits is verifiable only as strong conjecture. It is in the nature of reality to be subject to our fantasies about other people's conceptions of the world. My thoughts about Manuel and Jane might usefully be understood as nothing more than an alternate version of Manuel's thoughts about Jane and about Maria—Maria in relation to Bernhardt, though not exclusively in relation to Bernhardt. Rebecca had come swiftly and gracefully into the picture; and what you realized, listening to her talk or watching her throw up, was that, despite her youth, Rebecca was undeniably more grown-up than Leslie Constant. One glance at the Englishwoman in relation to Sherwin Lang made this clear. Leslie gazed across their table at Sherwin; she stared and stared. I think I can in fairness say that this was the finest and most alarming demonstration I've ever seen of the infant gaze in a non–mother/child setting. Who could blame the man for wanting to end it? He uncrossed his arms and placed his bottle beside all the others on the table. He slid back his chair, wiggling the chair's wooden legs across the floor, scuffing and scraping away from the trainee. Suddenly he leaned his body forward; and it looked as if he might speak to Leslie, perhaps whisper something sweet to placate her and make her smile. Instead he turned away. The man knew how to crush another person. Touching the tabletop with one hand, clutching his chair with the other, Lang worked himself to his feet. Each unsteady action was a considered, deliberate movement. What power this man had, drunk. He walked with care between tables, though he performed a kind of swaggering show to the contrary. Everyone in the room waited for Sherwin to tumble hilariously across someone's lap. But drunks have a knack for finding their way. And sure enough, here he came, weaving across the floor. I could see his enormous head, lit up and red in the bright kitchen light.

He seemed to be doing exactly what I had earlier warned Rebecca about—namely, spying up her dress.

Sherwin glared woozily up at us. He did not look well. He raved at the waitress, "Kernberg? Don't go to *Kernberg*! Kernberg is *haunted*! Everyone knows that. The place is crawling with ghosts of children who were forced to become musicians!"

Then he said, with the practiced alcoholic's sluggish though impeccable diction: "Don't listen to me. I am a stupid man. Sometimes I say harmless things. Give me your hand. Tom will not mind. I am sure of it. And Richard is strong. They are good men. They will understand. I cannot bear falling in love with a new woman."

He was so very, very drunk. There was no stopping him. He reached his hand up to Rebecca and, in a voice that was heartbreaking to hear, asked her, "Will you hold me?"

What was Rebecca to do? She looked at me, but I could not tell if it was guidance she wanted.

"Trust your instincts," I told her, and immediately felt like a manipulator and a fraud; for Rebecca must have known it was not likely that I would appreciate competition for her attention, especially from a charming drunk like Sherwin, who, regardless of his stated inclination to dodge the pains and sorrows of love, would waste no time getting his hands all over her tits. I couldn't alert Rebecca to this without coming off as a pig. I surely would've maneuvered to feel her breasts myself, if I could have gotten free from Bernhardt's grip. One day I will draft a paper on "Piety as an Expression of the Grotesque." I should say on this subject that my impression of myself as a fraud had certain cheery implications. The world's most accomplished charlatans—through no fault of their own—tend to be ordinary adolescents, who dedicate, on average, three to six years of their lives to creating, working through, and eventually discarding possible though often improbable personalities. We've all watched this process with the utmost horror. Did my own, calculated fraudulence indicate a highly compressed stage of psychological growth analogous to "normal" teen development? Was I, through these tender negotiations with Rebecca, leaving the state of infancy imposed by Bernhardt?

Oh, happiness! How glorious to become, over the course of a lifetime or a pancake dinner, a fabricator of deceits, a strategist in sex, the vanquisher of rivals—a true man, or at least a man who knows what it takes to look handsome, desirable, generous of spirit! Let Sherwin ascend into the air. Let him come up and take his place beside me and Rebecca. What did I have to fear from this unfortunate old friend, with his bloodshot eyes and comical, pseudo-Victorian costume?

Lang could only make me look good. I gave Rebecca the nod. To make sure she understood, I said, "Haul him up."

What was interesting to me was the sudden discovery that, having said this, I truly wanted it. I felt, as I frequently have in the past, a great, brokenhearted fondness for the man. It is not unusual to voice, as a prerequisite to articulating in consciousness, one's incipient and often strong desires, fears, hopes, misgivings, and so on. Rebecca was at that moment the person closest to me. I could feel heat from her body. I could smell her vomit. I felt her palm's moistness against mine. Was I in love with her? Was my attraction in some way paternalistic? She, too, apparently wanted Sherwin to float around the restaurant with us. Did the girl have a soft spot for drunks? If so, what might this suggest about her home life? And how did Bernhardt feel about the prospect of Sherwin leaning in and breathing beery breath everywhere? No one bothered to ask. Rebecca took the initiative and stuck out her free hand—it was her left—for Sherwin to grab. At the same time, with her lovely, damp right hand she gave my hand a light squeeze. She was letting me know that she was *with me,* and that this new connection with Sherwin was a connection she and I could build together. Bernhardt as well sensed that Sherwin's ascension was a meaningful testament to the bond between me and Rebecca, between himself and the two of us anchored in his embrace. The inclusion of Sherwin was a sign of our basic trust in one another's judgment relating to social life and the kind of company we valued and enjoyed. Sherwin was our kind of guy. Richard gave my ribs one of those tight, awful squeezes he liked to give whenever he wanted to communicate. I felt as if I were being squeezed all over. Bernhardt was squeezing, Rebecca was squeezing; everyone hugged and snuggled and perspired. I noticed, with pleasure and satisfaction, the pain in my chest, the sheer inability to breathe deeply. I gazed with pity at the world below. The analysts and the trainees around their messy tables seemed puny and mean, shabby, cut off from the love filling the top of the room above their heads.

Sherwin Lang, bleary, tall, dissolute Sherwin, fogged on beer among those disconsolate post-Freudians, swayed from side to side, unsteadily rocked. His face flushed red seemed longer and broader, more round and immense than it usually does; even his eyes, staring out wildly, had hardly any white showing. Rebecca lowered her finely made hand toward him—much as I, earlier in the evening, had reached with my own, larger and rougher hand for hers. Rebecca's arm in its blue gingham sleeve stretched down toward Sherwin; and the man's long arm, in black, scratchy wool, extended upward; and once again there was the impression—exactly as there had been when I made my move and lifted Rebecca from the ground—there was the impression of a great, barely traversable gulf between up here and down there.

Across this divide reached the arms of the girl and the man. Their fingers touched, their hands joined together. Sherwin started to rise. His face looked amazed. He went up on tiptoes. His pointy, mean-looking shoes left the floor, and Sherwin dangled above the tables spread with their blue cloths. His feet kicked and his body twirled this way and that as if pushed by wind. But there was no wind. We were indoors with the windows shut. The hospital's upper stories were approaching from the north, heading toward a late-night rendezvous with the Pancake House & Bar, though no one else noticed this. Everyone was focused on Sherwin in the air. The analysts and the students, even the lovesick teenagers, pushed back their chairs, slid sideways out from cramped booths, and came together in discrete, curious gangs near the fish tank or the candy display; they all gazed up and pointed at the hanging man; and it was, I thought then, as if these people had only that moment truly *realized* what was going on. But as we all know, awareness takes time.

Manuel and Maria and Peter, and the analytic trainees and Sherwin and Leslie, and Dan Graham and Terry, Elizabeth and Mike, and the lovesick youngsters and the waitresses wearing blue—the *group,* in other words—had begun to consciously acknowledge, *as* a group, as a society, that several of its members were in fact buzzing around, throwing up, chatting about life, and bumping into pots and pans overhead.

If only I could've wrapped my arms around Rebecca. That would have been sweet. There aren't many opportunities, as one gets on in life, to hug the young. The way things were going, with everybody watching us and pointing, and with Sherwin taking pains to come drunkenly aboard, Rebecca and I were not likely to get much privacy. It was a shame to lose this opportunity to snuggle with her.

Here came Lang. Damn him. I watched him learning to fly. It was a discouraging sight. Lang was clearly horrified at what was happening to him. He swung in the air beneath Rebecca. Perspiration caused his hair to flatten and adhere to his forehead. Fear and unhappiness could be read in his expression and his physical comportment (if Sherwin's movements could accurately be called that; "writhing" might be a better choice), in, it seemed to me, looking down from Bernhardt's arms, every aspect of Lang's Self and his being. What was the trouble? Rebecca tugged and pulled, and yet Lang remained, at least from my perspective, quite far beneath her, rising only slowly through the middle distance between the floor and the hanging garden of pots and skillets, between the people on earth and the people above the earth.

Down below Sherwin, analysts and the waitresses milled around like people doing—what? It was as if someone had gotten up from a booth and, in a startled and alarmed voice, exclaimed, "Look up there!," then pointed at something terrible. An airplane with flames trailing from the wing? A crash about to happen? The spirit of the party was changing, though it was hard to identify the nature or trajectory of the change. Was everyone waiting for a tragedy? (Another and perhaps more far-reaching question might be: What, specifically, was the tragedy that everyone was waiting for?) Dan Graham, wearing those cumbersome orthopedic shoes that feature one rubber sole piled thicker than the other, clumped between the tables and chairs, then stood leaning against the fish tank, puffing a filtered cigarette. He considered Lang. Dan looked, as always, lonely. Or he looked, I should say, wise. Smoke rose into the air and pooled beneath the ceiling. The reservoir of Dan's smoke grew; it was like an upside-down puddle, endlessly replenished from below by the man's exhalations, and by the gray, wet-looking stream that flowed from Dan's cigarette's tip. Was it a good idea for a man of Graham's size to rest his weight against a glass tank filled with water? Dan is a reasonably—no, more than reasonably—a thoroughly bright, insightful professional; he's published on topics relating to privacy and degradation in the analytic setting, and, more to the point in connection with Lang, on working with the recalcitrant substance abuser; certainly Dan's patients like and respect him; and I would have been interested in hearing his opinions on Sherwin's ascension, though I was not, I admit, thrilled with the prospect of dragging Dan up for a chat; he weighed, I would estimate, somewhere in the region of two hundred and thirty, maybe two hundred and fifty pounds.

Sherwin kicked and squirmed. A man hanged from the neck might struggle in the same fashion. Dan's lit cigarette stuck out from the corner of his mouth; the cigarette appeared to be growing there, a permanent, jittery, burning appendage rooted in Dan's beard. Ashes broke off and crumbled across the front of Dan's flannel shirt.

Then a woman—it sounded like Maria, yes, of course it was she; who else could it have been?—cried out, "Tom has gone too far this time! He's gone too *far*! He's absolutely *gone too far*!"

What was Maria blaming me for? Was everything my fault? Why was everything always my fault?

It wasn't like I'd spit water on anybody. I hadn't pulled a chair quickly, quietly from behind someone sitting down.

It was Bernhardt who had usurped our food, then squeezed the air out of my chest and gotten an erection that he shoved again and again against my back. I could feel it there, Bernhardt's hard-on rubbing away, poking me, as people on the ground pointed up at Lang in his strange coat, Lang drunkenly flying toward Rebecca's embrace.

Watching Sherwin clutch the waitress's hand, I was put in mind of hapless men carried aloft on anchor lines trailing from balloons or airships torn from their moorings, swiftly ascending.

If Sherwin were to release Rebecca's hand, if he panicked and fell, would the charismatic, womanizing psychiatrist then plummet to his death amid bread crumbs and soiled napkins dropped like so many ladies' handkerchiefs on the Pancake House floor?

Or might he, following the style of some exhibition diver executing a circus stunt, get lucky and cannonball past Dan Graham's head, into the tropical aquarium bubbling beside the cash register?

"Hold Rebecca's hand! You can make it! Don't look at the ground!" I called to Lang. He twisted desperately.

Rebecca cautioned the thrashing man, "Stop fighting! You'll make me drop you! There's nothing to be afraid of!"

In fact there was something to be afraid of. There was Leslie Constant, barging furiously through the crowd.

"Come down here, Sherwin Lang! Don't fly off without me! Don't you dare leave me all alone down here with these *horrible* child psychologists! Come back to the table and drink another beer, will you? Sherwin! Let me bring you a cold ale! You *bastard*! You don't know how to treat a woman! I don't care if you do have a medical degree! All American men are exactly alike! That's *right*! You don't any single one of you know how to *spoil* your women! You're all so fucking *cheap*! I pity American women for having to live with you their *whole lives*! You can't even buy a girl *dinner*—you have to go to some *breakfast* place where there's nothing to eat except *fried bread*! All this sugar makes me *ill*! Do you hear me? Do you *hear* me, Sherwin? And it's always *someone else* picking up the check! Isn't that true? Don't fly away from me, *Doctor* Lang! Oh, you'll do anything to get out of spending *money*! Sherwin, don't leave me! Don't go away—*oh, you*!" And so on, cursing and shoving her way between people, jostling them aside, finally plowing between Maria and Escobar, out into the open circle beneath her brilliant, drunken, levitating paramour. Leslie was a little shaky, off balance on a pair of startlingly tall navy-blue spike heels that went very nicely with her knee-length navy skirt and white silk blouse. I had not noticed the shoes earlier, when Leslie had been sitting with legs tucked beneath her table. Had she been drinking beer at the same rate as Sherwin? Was Leslie drunk? The fact that this woman was a native of the British Isles argued, to my mind, in favor of the possibility. Probably I should not say a thing like that about the English or anyone else. It's a slur and, as such, expresses the kind of derisive stereotype that will surely be found offensive by some, no doubt about it; but the fact remains that the English, the Irish, and, I suppose, the Scottish and the Welsh—am I leaving anybody out?— stereotypically or not, have a long, colorful history of problems with alcohol. Who can study their literature, much less look at their art, and deny this?

Leslie wobbled into position beneath Sherwin. You could see her eyes following her swinging man, this way, that way, like the eyes of a person watching tennis from center court. And, watching Leslie, with her blond hair cut short, her subtle, Anglican nose, her intent gaze, I was put in mind of our cat at home, Lawrence Mandelbaum, stalking, from the Persian rug in the living room, a catnip string toy held teasingly overhead—you never know when the cat will swat. I held tightly to Rebecca, and I felt Bernhardt adjust his grip around me: we were a team: we did not need to discuss matters. Together we braced to handle Sherwin, struggling and kicking in the space between Rebecca and Leslie.

"Don't let him get away!" shouted a man in the crowd. It was Mike Breuer, who all along had understood the essential *rightness* of Leslie and his friend joined in matrimony or at least in some temporary congress.

"Jump!" another voice called, from over near the bar. The speaker this time was young. Was it the teenage boy, recklessly getting in on the adult action? I felt that there was the potential for mob behavior. Everyone was roving around looking for something to do. It was that late, disheartening time in the evening when, at a different sort of party, dancing begins.

Sure enough, Konwicki's child psychologists took up the chant. "Jump. Jump. Jump."

What would Leslie do? She watched Sherwin swinging like a crazy pendulum over her. Leslie's high heels gave her stature. She could easily reach up and grab Lang's trouser cuffs, then climb his clothes, grasp him by the belt, and circle her arms around his waist. That was not, however, what she did. She reached up with one pale white arm and, in a move that showed, as they might put it in the sports world, athletic ability, caught one of Lang's flying balmoral shoes, bare-handed. There was a sound not unlike the sound made by a hard-hit line drive landing in an outfielder's mitt. *Thwack.* She held him by the foot. "Got you!" she proclaimed in her London accent, the emphasis heavily on "got," which sounded like "gaught."

A cheer went up. "Way to catch! Excellent snatch!" shouted the teenager. This kid, I could tell, was going to become a nuisance before long. But what could I do about it? He had his arm wrapped around his girlfriend's shoulders; they leaned into one another in that suggestive, suffocating way that kids will when in public, in order to let the unhappy adult world know that they sleep together for fun. I was high in the air, looking down and holding with all my might to the chain of humanity.

I could tell from Bernhardt's breathing, his rapid, short gasps, that the new people were putting a strain on him. Leslie's feet came off the floor. Her blue high heels dangled from her toes. People gathered in a close circle beneath her, side-coaching her to snag Sherwin's other shoe and hoist herself up, to lock her arms around his ankles.

"The shoe is coming in on your left! Behind you! Wait until the shoe is in front of you! You want to make eye contact with the shoe! Don't take your eyes off the shoe!" Mike called to Leslie. With his balding head and his wide, tooth-filled mouth, and wearing his plaid polo shirt precisely tucked into pleated, high-waisted pants, he looked to me like a study of a

Little League dad. "I'll tell you when to move. Ready? Here comes the shoe. It's almost there. *Now.*"

Leslie swept the air with her free hand, but missed the black shape darting alongside her face.

"Anticipate!" Mike yelled angrily. Then he recovered composure and explained, in tones that perfectly blended exasperation with patience, "Your hand must *go* to the place where the shoe will *be.*"

Again Lang's shoe swung past Leslie, and again she tried and failed to catch it. Lang's shoe moved through the air as if it had a life and a mind all its own. With one hand, Leslie gripped Lang's other foot. How long could she hold on? The man tried to shake the woman loose. I couldn't watch what was happening. I worried for Leslie. Would it be somehow fitting, I wondered, for Sherwin Lang, the veteran alcoholic, the skirt chaser, to inadvertently, fiercely kick a woman in love?

This probability made me afraid.

Sherwin, stretched between Rebecca above and Leslie below, appeared to me to embody, in his concrete, physical situation, the classic predicament of a man devoted to seduction.

"Help me! For God's sake! I don't want to die like this!" he called out to no one and everyone, as the Englishwoman, in a courageous show of endurance and youthful exuberance, dragged herself up and began the difficult ascent of his leg.

"Don't let go of my hand!" ordered Rebecca. Was she screaming at Lang or at me? Sherwin seemed more than ever to hang from a great and unsafe height.

And my friends on the ground had become, during the time while these things were taking place, farther and farther away. They receded, Dan and Elizabeth and the rest, and became, it seemed, tinier and tinier in size. This had been happening all night long. It was part of the whole psychic hallucination experience. It was as though the restaurant's ceiling were continually, unstoppably rising. Up we went, the waitress and I, following beneath the pots and the bright, hot lights—and with us came Lang and Leslie strung out from our arms. And yet, even as we soared, I could see, as I had all evening, looking down at my earthbound peers—I could make out, in gross detail, people's clothes and their hairstyles, their eyeglasses and the pens jammed into their pockets, and their watery eyes and skin blemishes and the outlines of veins running beneath the skin, all the movements and tics made by their faces changing expression, the minor though distinguishing material characteristics of their personalities.

I could hear their cries, their criticisms and whispers, including Peter Konwicki's confidential speculations to his students gazing at Leslie clawing her way up Sherwin.

"Look closely," the feral man said to the trainees, who hung, as they say, on his every word. "You'll never witness a more dramatic instance of female sexual acquisitiveness."

"It's remarkable what people will do in order to procreate, isn't it?" said Bob, Konwicki's A student. The girl beside Bob, the girl named Katharine (who had earlier predicted, in a casual, offhand style, that my personal situation indicated a reorientation of sexual identity and a subsequent repudiation of socially binding mores . . . well, maybe—what about it?), commented, "I saw something like this on one of those television nature programs."

"Was that the documentary on Madagascar, by any chance?" asked Bob.

"Madagascar? It might've been."

"With the tree lemurs? Were there tree lemurs?"

"Tree lemurs? Yes. I believe there were tree lemurs. Do they have the pink noses and the incredibly long tails?"

"I don't know about their noses," Bob pronounced in deep, resonant tones. He sounded as if he were laying claim to something—as if he were really saying, "This discussion belongs to me." In this spirit, and not unlike a hypnotist working a charm, he now intoned, "Their tails are long. Their tails are very long."

"I remember the lemurs' tails," sighed the girl trainee. She was helping Bob by deliberately—or maybe unconsciously—acting dreamy, assuming the subordinate position and letting the young man effectively take possession of her intellectual property: it was, after all, she, not he, who had made the connection between Lang, Leslie, and a nature documentary.

At this point Bob stepped up and threw what I thought was a risky pitch. "Lemurs have sex all the time. They're completely promiscuous. They have sex with their own relatives. They're known to masturbate again and again. They're just constantly having sex."

The girl stayed silent. Had Bob played things too hard, too fast? Had he revealed himself to be erotically suspect? Apparently these considerations were immaterial to Katharine. She lowered her head in a manner that can best be described as girlish. She peeked around to see who, if anyone, might be watching. She rested her shoulder against Bob's arm. She was ready to give herself to him.

And so it went. The heavy fog closed in. The rain approached. The city disappeared and the hospital came closer. Bob had Katharine. Leslie had Lang. Maria had Richard. Richard had me. Manuel had my wife. The teenagers had each other. Peter had his students and Elizabeth had Mike and Mike had his kids at home. Terry Kropp was new at the Insti tute; I knew nothing about him. Dan Graham had, I guess, his cigarettes.

I clutched Rebecca's hand. In the air, everyone held someone. I watched Rebecca support Lang, who panicked and kicked as Leslie Constant climbed his leg to couple with him. I knew then that Rebecca was undeniably, immutably a Krakower Institute Young Woman of Strength.

Was it too much to hope that we might fly out of here—Rebecca and I, straight out a window or through the Pancake House roof together? Might we (if we tried hard—if, like a made-up boy and girl in a children's storybook, we *wished* hard), might we escape this circus scene, this lovelorn human ladder, and instead blast off, break free from the clamorous mob, and penetrate, swiftly, the restaurant's ceiling, the white tiles and the hardwood beams, the pink insulation and the heavy, noxious tar paper on top? I knew exactly where I'd want to go with Rebecca. Battlefield Grove. That's right. The primitive burial mound with the Revolutionary War cannon pointed from the low hills to fire on its sacred graves. We'd want to carry a blanket—a blue polyester-blend tablecloth might work—to spread over the ground or wrap ourselves against the night air. Maybe Rebecca would be willing to swoop down and grab a thermos of coffee or tea on the way out. If Bernhardt might kindly loosen his grip, I could possibly manage to reach into my pocket and take out the five-, ten-, and twenty-dollar bills crumpled there, let these drop from my fingers like leaves that would flutter down and settle across the cash-register keys—or if I aimed poorly and missed, the money would fall into the aquarium and get wet, but who cares?—just so that there would be no disputes over the bill. Then off we'd go.

First we'd climb above the fog. Elevation is key. Flying, even the kind of "out-of-body" projection that Rebecca and I would be doing—that she and I were already doing—could, one imagines, be hazardous without clement weather and long-range visibility. This is a technical matter, but it is not strictly, or merely, technical; the psychological ramifications of slamming into a tree or a building are daunting to consider, under any circumstances. In order not to consider them, we would soar above the mist.

How lovely to be in the clear night where no one is smoking cigarettes or eating eggs! I'd have to remember to ask Bernhardt to shift his arms again, just a bit, to take the pressure off my ribs, so that I might suck a clean, wintry breath of air into my lungs. A deep breath. Unfortunately, I don't know much about the stars in their constellations, so I couldn't name any for Rebecca. That would not stop us from admiring the Milky Way's brilliance, or, alternatively, from enjoying a periodic glimpse, a mile or so beneath us, of flat water, our river coursing serpentine across the land, snaking east and south, reflecting occasional moonlight that falls in broken columns through windblown openings in the clouds.

If you follow the river, you'll come to the battlefield. Rebecca and I go, as the counterculture used to put it, with the flow, tilting our heads to the right and consequently soaring right, leaning to port and sailing gently left. Vigorous motion either way results in rolling. Rebecca and I somersault for fun. We're showing off! I don't like too much twirling, because—I should know this by now—it makes me sick to my stomach. She, I am sure, feels the same way. "Let's take it easy," I say to her, and in unison we tip back our heads in calculated imitation of the voluntary backward pull you will make when sitting in a rapidly decelerating vehicle. This slows our speed. Now and again a dot or beam of light appears below, and Rebecca and I know we are passing over a house where people are awake, or a car driven along a country lane by someone going home late.

Is it possible that Jane sits clutching the wheel inside one of these cars, our green sedan creeping south through fog along Eureka Drive, past the book factory and down the hill, through the covered bridge and around the old airport, coming to fetch me home after my long night out flirting, arguing, and flying?

What will Jane do when she arrives at the Pancake House to find me gone, risen through the roof beams? Might she take off her coat, relax at a table, nibble a muffin, and chat—casually, as if there were nothing going on between the two of them—with Escobar?

Rebecca and I lean forward in the breeze above the road, repositioning our heads and tucking in chins to streamline for speed. The city is behind us. Rebecca's hair falls across her shoulders; it blows back in the wind, and I am able for a brief instant to see Brueghel's dog grinning at me from her neck, and naturally I wonder what this dog wants to tell me.

Ahead lies Battlefield Grove. There's the burial mound, a grass circle that looks to be, ironically, about the diameter of a cannonball, viewed from on high. Rebecca and I try to avoid knocking into each other as we buzz around checking for a landing place away from trees. I should say that we try to give one another the impression that we are physically avoidant, and in the process collide many times. What is more pleasurable than inadvertent bumping? We're already holding hands; now I put my arm around her—neither too tentatively nor too confidently. A slight, half-baked hug is all I can attempt. It's enough. Rebecca feels safe and, although she does not register this immediately, turned on. I tell myself that what I really want is to take care of her, to be the kind of adult she can lean on, to help her separate from her family and get a better job and decide which courses to take in college.

But if this is the case, if my most ardent desire is to counsel and protect, then why am I luring Rebecca to the burial mound, a known make-out destination?

The grass is cushiony. It is long and uncut, matted and bowed over, a meadow in a cold season. I realize, touching down to earth, that it has been a long time—ever since Bernhardt picked me up and forced me to drop the cinnamon-raisin toast—a long time since I stood unsupported on the ground. My toes touch, and I feel the grass compress underneath me. I am wearing understated dress shoes with leather soles and modest arch support, and I am surprised, initially, at the leather's capacity for transmission of sensation: as my feet land, I comprehend the earth in detail. From beneath the grass stalks, hidden from sight, rocks and other surface irregularities impress themselves against my shoe's soles; and when my body's weight bears down, the rocks dig in. I shift and compensate, moving my left foot left, my right to the right; curling, then stretching, my toes and pushing up from the balls of my feet. I stand. A stick cracks beneath my heel, and I become conscious of the first waves of pain traveling down from my lower back, through my pelvis and along the sciatic pathway into my legs. How obvious. Something like this could only be expected after hours spent weightless, the long night in close embrace with Bernhardt. And, undoubtedly, there is a powerful psychological component. The logic of pain, though emotional and, arguably, sentimental, is rudimentary. The pain originates in my lumbar area. This is where, on Jane's back, the fishermen made of birthmarks survey the horizon from their tiny wooden boats. And it is, on my back, the place where Bernhardt's erection has been pressing against me; and, really, I think—I can say this as a professional, not just as a sufferer—it's impossible to underestimate the effect of an intrusive penis in relation to somatized sciatica. Whatever the etiology, I must acknowledge that the spasms make me want to drop to my knees and cry like a baby. I've had lower back symptoms before, but never like this, never so piercing and extreme. It is fortunate—and so *like* her—that Rebecca is beside me. I have my arm draped partway around her waist, and she herself is coming to rest, sinking down in grass that bends and crunches underfoot. Her hip brushes against mine, and her leg touches my leg, and she eases down next to me, and we huddle together at the center of the sacred mound.

(About the people who dug this primeval monument, little is known save that they were prehistoric and almost certainly nomadic—no sites resembling this one have been discovered elsewhere in the vicinity—a tall and long-limbed folk who used the most primitive stone tools, and who predate by many ages the more recent Native American tribes, the Seminoles and the Cherokee dynasty that occupied the southern and mid-Atlantic territories, the Iroquois and the Huron societies in the North, and the countless autonomous nations between, whose warriors were on hand to greet the European explorers and settlers in the late fifteenth through the early seventeenth centuries. Perhaps the builders of the mound were outcasts from a loosely organized civilization that may, as some believe, have come to fruition, then mysteriously disappeared, in the West and Midwest, thousands of years ago. Whoever they were, it invariably gives me a bit of a sexual thrill—I'm not certain I should be admitting this—to march around on top of their skeletons.)

"Ow! My back! Ow! Ow!"

Marching is out of the question. I'm shaky, more than a little wobbly; and Rebecca, seeing me in trouble, perceiving my affliction, wraps my arm tightly around her shoulders and, holding my hand in hers, taking a tiny step forward, says, "I'll help you walk."

So, of course, it is she helping me, and not the other way

around as I had wished—or as I had thought I wished. Because, you see, it may also be true that I am, in my infirmity, in my inability to walk without assistance, at last getting what I need and want.

Together we shuffle around the mound. Each step becomes an act of falling over onto Rebecca; and with each step I feel a dagger plunged in my spine at exactly Bernhardt's cock's point of contact. "Jesus!" I exclaim as the blade goes in. Rebecca carries the thermos and the blue tablecloth. We take turns drinking coffee or tea or whatever she's brought, sipping from the plastic cup that doubles as a thermos lid; and I make up for my ignorance regarding astronomy and the galaxies by gamely pointing out historic sights, more or less invisible in the night and the fog, though still vaguely distinguishable, here and there.

"A tattered and exhausted detachment of colonials camped here briefly during the winter in 1775," I inform her, nodding my head gingerly to indicate the area over which she, leaving me to wait uncomfortably, precariously on my own two feet, spreads her blue tablecloth. I lean over, bend my legs, and place my hands on my knees, taking the weight off my back. Rebecca's tablecloth, it turns out, is enormous, many times larger than might be expected if seen draped over a Pancake House & Bar table. There is room on the open cloth to lie down and stretch out, or to pace back and forth, or even run around in a circle: it's that big.

I grit my teeth against a succession of bad muscle tremors. I tell Rebecca, "At the time of the War of Independence, this was no grove. Only a few significant old-growth woodlands were to be found in the entire county. Rural land around here was cleared for farms in the eighteenth century. It was sheep country. Hardwoods were used for cooking and building and heating. By the late nineteenth century, the eastern North American forests had been burned up in fireplaces."

"What a waste," Rebecca might say in response, expressing the kind of modern ecological values that colonial settlers could neither have imagined nor afforded.

Under the circumstances—the night air's sweetness; the smoky smell in Rebecca's hair; the little dog's ostensibly meaningful grin; the agony that comes with standing, learning to walk, feeling tiny rocks bite through my shoes into my feet, etc.—I consider it wise to steer away from the complexities of land management and environmental preservation. "At any rate, the minutemen camped here. A party of redcoats transporting light artillery were at that time bivouacked adjacent to the post road"—pointing and gesturing toward the far distance, though in fact nothing more than thirty feet away is discernible in the mist, or so it seems—"over beyond those hills. On the morning of the engagement, the British, led not by General John Burgoyne, incidentally, as some of the local Revolutionary War buffs like to think, but by a commissioned officer who afterward drowned during a river crossing—and while I'm at it, let me just add, Rebecca, that, whatever Dr. Woody might have taught you in eleventh grade, and whatever the plaques put up by the Parks Department would have us believe, General Burgoyne never rode through these parts. Anyone who claims he did is critically misinformed. Burgoyne was on a man-o'-war, sailing home across the Atlantic to plan the campaign of Saratoga—anyway, for what it's worth, the British were under the command of a young lieutenant who was fated to fall through the ice several days after the so-called Incident on the Mound. So, okay, that's neither here nor there. On the morning of the fight, which really wasn't much of a fight, you know, in the end, and that's the interesting part, on the morning of the fight, just before sunrise, the British hauled their fieldpieces over those hilltops"—once again pointing, for no good reason, into the invisible East— "placing them behind earthworks hastily dug into the hills facing the American encampment."

"What are earthworks?" Rebecca asks me. I can't tell if she is genuinely interested or if she is humoring me.

"Earthworks are barriers designed to protect the cannon and the soldiers responsible for aiming and firing."

"That makes sense," answers Rebecca, smoothing a corner of the enormous blue cloth.

"But it was winter and the ground was frozen. The infantry were unable to heap up more than a few spadefuls of dirt, and for this reason their defenses were inadequate."

"That's too bad," says Rebecca, predictably voicing, on this occasion, the sort of irritatingly provocative, politically contrarian position—a typical young person's stance, commending our national enemies, the English, at a defining moment in the nation's birth—a position that, notwithstanding virtues it may possess in the abstract, is, like contemporary ecological radicalism, explicitly a derivative of the most up-to-date, democratic potentials in society, the very potentials, one might add, that the British under their insane monarch were fighting to suppress.

I don't bother, while standing bent over on the mound, to discuss the psychopathology of aggression with Rebecca.

I notice that she has reclined on the tablecloth. She has left me alone with my back pain. Rebecca lies on her side, sipping from the thermos lid, watching me from the cloth's other end. To reach her, I must travel a great distance across a soft blue expanse.

Has the time come at last for me to fall down on my knees? It has, and I do it; I tip forward with hands outstretched and let gravity move me. My knees hit the ground first, followed by hands; and the grass underneath the cloth absorbs the impact of knees and hands, the unavoidable shock to the body; and, surprisingly, my fall is cushioned and painless, which is to say that falling does not bring new pain. It feels to me as if a giant blue mattress has been unfurled across the top of the prehistoric mound.

I'm on all fours, as they say. Rebecca waits in the mist. Am I wrong to imagine that we may soon be making love on our blue bed? What will this be like? Will Rebecca act shy and insecure? Will I? Might she, in the manner of a woman with experience, know what to do and how to do it? Our first kiss will be the answer to these questions.

I can see her up ahead, though she is quickly fading from view in the fog that grows thicker and thicker.

I set out crawling. My progress is slow. The ground is cold. I keep my back low; it is best if I do not use my legs in any way; rather, I prefer to drag them behind me, because I have lost feeling in my feet. My body seems to end at some undetermined point below the hips. Yet I have weight. I clutch folds of blue tablecloth in my hands, plant my elbows, and, keeping in mind the restrictions imposed by Richard's hug—for I remain, even while snaking across the mound, effectively trapped back at the Pancake House & Bar, a prisoner, strait-jacketed in Bernhardt's embrace—I work myself forward. Rocks scrape me as I pass over the cloth. I will surely have bruises. I feel that I am scaling a mountain or a lengthy, graded hill, which in a fashion I am; the burial mound forms a rounded slope that, for a legless man, becomes a challenging and demanding ascent. I am like a soldier maimed in battle, worming toward safety and trying not to die. This imagery of disablement is not inappropriate, I think, given the history of the location; given, as well, my physical situation vis-à-vis Bernhardt, etc., that night at the Pancake House. Out here in Battlefield Grove, my comprehension of safety—this for reasons having more to do with solace than with sex—is bound up with reaching Rebecca. As I squirm toward the vanishing girl, I describe to her, in a loud voice that I can only hope she hears, events as they took place in the winter of 1775, the Incident on the Mound.

"The British artillery company unlimbered their big muzzle-loaders and positioned them on the hillsides. The Americans were asleep in their tents. English infantry filed down the hills and assembled ranks. It was customary in that age for attacking armies to progress while firing at the enemy from overlapping lines, one kneeling and one standing, in broad daylight, while wearing bright jackets."

Sticks and rocks abrade my elbows. My back is bathed in a warm, excruciating pain.

I struggle up the mound. I can no longer see Rebecca. The

mist has shrouded her; night draws toward dawn, and dew on grass under the tablecloth soaks through. My clothes are drenched.

"At daybreak the English cannon opened fire. *Kablam! Kablam!*"—here I pause, after making the slightly ridiculous, expletive cannon sounds, to cough a few times. "The noise was deafening. Explosions echoed from hill to hill. Flashes from the gun barrels lit the sky. Cannon shot flew through the air toward the helpless Americans."

"What happened?" asks the disembodied, excited voice of Rebecca. I am glad to hear her. She can't be far away.

"The artillery roared. The infantry advanced. Suddenly a thick fog settled over the land."

"Like the fog now?" asks Rebecca from somewhere inside the dense, ground-level clouds.

"Yes. A fog came down, a fog like this one, obscuring the mound and the colonial soldiers."

"Wow."

"The English artillery fired and fired, but not a single shot found its target. The infantry fixed bayonets and charged, but at the last instant became confused in the mist and went astray to the south. Each man lost contact with the man next to him. Panicked regulars struck out at whatever moved. A blind skirmish took place. Redcoats attacked redcoats. I know because I was there. I played the role of the drowned lieutenant one year during the winter battle re-enactment."

"You did?" asks Rebecca, suddenly perking up. "My father used to participate in the enactments. He stopped doing it when I was eleven."

"Your father? How about that. What army was your father in?"

"British, like you. That depressed him. Dad never, ever talks about the battle. He had a bad experience."

"What happened?"

"Somebody stabbed him with a bayonet."

"Hmm."

"What's wrong?"

What to say? What to do? Tell the truth and endure the consequences? Act like nothing is amiss, and risk later disclosures of crucial, compromising omissions?

I take the high road, like a man. "I don't quite know how to tell you this, Rebecca, but—let me think about the right way to say this—uh, if your father is who I think he is, what I'm trying to say is, I may have—how do I want to put this?—I may have accidentally bayoneted him."

"Oh my God."

"Rebecca, I'm sorry. I didn't mean to do it. Please try to understand. We didn't have any rehearsals. The whole re-enactment was miserably organized. I hate guns."

"You bayoneted my father?"

"It was an accident. We ran into each other and my gun was pointed the wrong way and the bayonet got in the way and he got cut."

"You bayoneted my father. Oh my God. You bayoneted my father."

"I feel terrible about this, Rebecca."

"I can't believe it. You bayoneted Dad! And I *trusted* you," declares the girl—brilliantly commandeering, in the way offended people so frequently will, events that occurred years in the past, using them as retrospective evidence pertaining to present circumstances.

I have nothing to say to this illogical formulation except the tried and true "Can you forgive me? Rebecca? Can you find it in your heart to forgive me?"

"I *trusted* you!"

A moment passes while no one speaks and I wait to learn which way the wind blows. During this time I am able to ponder the significant implications. For better or for ill, Rebecca and I are bonded through the wounds of her father. It is not unheard-of for people to develop strong attachments to those who have harmed them, or, as in the current instance, to those who injure their loved ones.

With this in mind, and in order to take command of the situation, I ease into a calm and professional, sympathetic mode. "It must have been difficult for you, at such a young age, to see your father walk in the door all smeared with his own blood."

"It was. It was awful. I thought he was going to die," she remembers, quietly; and I coach her to observe these feelings and her childhood memories. "I'll understand if you're angry with me, Rebecca. I don't want to stand in the way of your sorrow."

"When Dad came home from the war, I cried and cried. He said he was fine and there was nothing to worry about, but I thought he was only telling me that so I wouldn't be sad about him dying."

Dying?

"Let me get this straight. Are you saying that the fact that your father was *not dying* convinced you he was?"

"What?" she says. Then, presumably, the semantics of the question sort themselves out in her head, and she answers, "I guess that's right. It doesn't make much sense, does it?"

"It makes perfect sense."

"I cried all night long."

"Do you feel like crying now?"

"No, why would I cry now? That's silly. I was eleven years old. I don't want to cry now."

I can't see Rebecca, though I can hear her, through the mist, breathing. I choose my next words with care. "Sometimes people bottle up their feelings, and years go by, and those repressed feelings can cause neurotic depressions and resentment." ·

"Oh, please. Don't be so condescending. I'm not one of your patients."

"I just thought I'd mention it."

"Dad wasn't hurt badly. Everything was better in the morning. He let me help with his bandages."

"How nice for both of you," I say to her. It's a tactical error, and I am immediately aware of it as such; I sound petulant and mean—I *am* petulant and mean. She of course hears the jealousy in my voice. "You're mad at me, aren't you?" she says.

"No," I lie.

"Why are you mad at *me*? I'm not the one who goes around sticking people with bayonets. You want me weepy like a little girl, because you can't deal with me as a woman."

"Hey! Hey!" is all I can manage to reply. Because of course she is indicting me for a legitimate reason.

In a voice that sounds very much like a woman's, in that it is deep and resonant with self-possession, with, I suppose I would say, feminine dignity and sexuality—not at all a girl's voice—she offers, "Why don't you tell me about the War Against the Crown, Tom?"

"Rebecca, we don't have to talk about the Revolutionary War if it makes you unhappy."

"I don't mind."

"Maybe it would be better not to."

"I want to."

In this way, together, we struggle, offering little concessions, trying carefully to establish good faith.

And I am cheered by her use, in such unaffected, relaxed style, of my name. She has acknowledged our connection. Is it decadent for me to feel optimistic about things? We are entering a new, more mature stage in our relationship.

There is, however, little more of interest to relate about the Incident on the Mound. The Americans were able to muster themselves and retreat without casualties. They stormed the frozen emplacements and captured the undefended six-pounder guns.

"That was the end of the battle?"

"Pretty much."

"It wasn't a major event, was it?" Rebecca asks me. I can tell from her voice that she is disappointed. Who could blame her for feeling this way? I can also tell that she is close at hand. I have made it, or almost made it, across the giant tablecloth.

All I need to do is reach up and fumble around until—I hope—I touch her; then, if feelings are mutual, and if she truly does not hate me for stabbing her dad; if, as is quite possible and in fact perversely likely in a situation like this, she in some way, perhaps without knowing it, loves me for slicing up her old man, we will embrace and, wrapping the cloth around us for a blanket, watch the sunrise and, in some probably limited way that gently and affectionately takes into account the loss of my legs, Rebecca and I will cuddle on this sacred earth.

I wiggle closer to her. I know she is near. It is touching to listen to Rebecca's breaths. The pursuit of the mound's summit has exhausted me. I am depleted, a cripple. In spite of the April night's cold, my face and back are damp with sweat. But what the wetness feels like to me is blood.

It hurts to breathe. I clutch the blue fabric laid so neatly by Rebecca across the meadow grass, and I tell her, in panting, half-delirious tones, a few entertaining facts about military provisioning and outfitting in the era of mad King George. Particularly noteworthy were the uniforms, which came complete with a tight, double-breasted tunic designed to button up and look smart on the parade ground, but which allowed for precious little movement of the upper body or arms. On behalf of her father, and to relieve my obvious sense of guilt, I denigrate the coats to Rebecca.

"They were straitjackets."

Then I tell her, "Your dress and this tablecloth are the identical shade of blue worn by American officers in the War for Independence."

"So?"

She's got me. What is the point I am trying to make?

Everything runs together and collides in my mind. Redcoats? Blue cloth? Guns blazing? Sticks and stones?

The hospital in the clouds. Sweat and blood. A little dog and the fishermen in their boats.

I am after all a married though childless man. I have a lot of problems. I have an unpainted room at the top of the stairs. I feel the dread of love. Jane wants our room blue.

Blue for a boy! Soul of my unborn son! The cloth on the mound! The waitress in her blue dress and Bernhardt wearing red, and the sweetness of pancakes and pitchers of milk and beer in bottles, and Sherwin Lang and all our old, tired heads going bald, and a hard-on pressing against my back, a man's arms wrapped around me.

General Burgoyne. Jane upstairs walking barefoot, the cat rubbing against her leg. Fog like a white smoke pooled beneath the sky.

"The fog that winter morning in 1775 was no accident, Rebecca. That bad weather came for a reason. I realize it may sound intemperate of me to say this, but I believe that the souls who reside in this grove will brook no violence against their resting place, nor against the living who seek asylum in the magic circle inscribed by the mound."

"Do you believe that?"

It's a good question. I'm not sure I can give an answer. Instead, I reach out with my hand and, without much trouble, find Rebecca's in the mist. My hand goes to hers. We are united. Holding Rebecca's warm fingers laced between mine, I am able to breathe more freely, and to stop thinking so hard about death. I feel soothed, a little.

It is at this moment that rain, having stayed in the distance, in the background as it were, for such a long time, for the duration of the night practically, begins to fall. I wrench my body forward—an ultimate, slightly dizzying effort to move before, finally, I am able to rest my head in Rebecca's lap. Rain strikes my shirt and the tablecloth, making its muted, intermittent noise, precipitation hitting fabric. Closing my eyes, I say to Rebecca, "The spirits of the dead are everywhere around us. They're out here now. Can you hear? We're not alone. Listen. The dead have come out to make love on the mound. Do you hear?"

"You're crazy," she says; and I murmur to her, "The spirits want us to love each other."

"No, they don't."

"Yes, they do."

"They don't."

"They do."

"No. They *don't!*" she insists.

"I'm afraid they do, actually, Rebecca," I say to her, shamelessly keeping to my line of seduction, adding physical emphasis by pressing and rubbing my forehead against her kneecap. She giggles, "You're being silly."

She's right. The question "How can I possibly speak with authority in a situation defined and permeated by sexual fantasy?" might better be asked: "How can I invoke ghosts as an excuse to come on to Rebecca, and keep a straight face?"

She says, "You're the kind of man who knifes someone's father and makes him bleed."

True enough. What can I say? I say what I can and put her on the defensive. "I've apologized for that already."

"I know. I'm sorry for bringing it up."

Then I say, making a subtly infantilizing, reciprocal conversational offering, "Don't apologize. You did nothing wrong."

She answers this with a question that breaks my heart:

"Do you love me?"

"You know I do," I tell her in genuinely sincere though deliberately evasive and ambiguous language.

It is then, of course, that I become *fully and absolutely aware* that Rebecca and I are not alone atop the sacred burial mound. And I must, under these circumstances, wonder if it is in fact possible that my "invocation" of accompanying, companionable, love-bound spirits could advantageously be understood as a spoken expression of personal and powerful creative agency. Have I become, as earlier in the evening I imagined I might, an inventor of reality? Have I, over the course of our long night in the Pancake House (and, for the sake of argument, out here on the ancient mound), become a child in the truest, most magical sense? Let us keep in mind that the flight to Battlefield Grove with Rebecca was nothing more than an elaborate and, admittedly, rather consuming fantasy; the whole thing has been entirely—or at least mostly: even the most transparently erotic fever dreams contain and reflect meaningful aspects of privileged, private emotional knowledge—the whole thing has been entirely, as I was say-ing, made up; our time together on the mound has existed (and, in a way, continues to function) in my head, in my mind; it was (and is) a subjective concoction, in other words; the flight to the mound was (is) simply what I'd *wished* (and will always and forevermore wish?) to be happening, though I cannot (I could not) in honesty claim that any of it *was* (or even *is*) happening, because—let's not forget—in reality, I was hanging like a doll from Bernhardt's massive arms, queasily drifting beneath the Pancake House ceiling with—let's not overlook this, either—my father figure's penis hard against my back, pressing, as they say, *into* my back; and, in uninvented reality, Rebecca also was suspended in air, dangling between me and my buddy Sherwin, holding both our hands, the doctor somewhat restrained in movement by his constricting black coat, nonetheless struggling drunkenly as Leslie Constant swung from his narrow belt like a trapeze girl about to lose her blue shoes. And in reality, Dan Graham was smoking a cigarette and propping his awkward weight against the decorative, bubbling fish tank, threatening to overturn the tank and flood the Pancake House. Behind the candy counter, Peter Konwicki's child-psychology trainee Bob slipped pink hands beneath Katharine's blouse, slipped them up and under her shirtfront's ruffled, untucked tail, feeling his classmate's stomach above her pants in a manner that he apparently thought unobtrusive to Katharine and unnoticeable to people standing nearby or hanging amid pots and pans overhead. These are—I should say these *were,* that April night of flapjacks and toast—a random assortment of substantive realities. These were not mere interpretations of feelings (I'm with Winnicott on the relative inconsequentiality of interpretations, either in the analytic setting or in everyday life); these were the couplings and levitations that I saw and felt and experienced. In spite of them, in spite of and because of every great and humiliating thing taking place that evening, I felt my head nestle into Rebecca's comfortable lap, and I heard the first spring shower fall onto Battlefield Grove, the rain coming down to spatter us; and I could smell ozone brought down by this weather, and the rich, virtually barnlike scent of fermenting winter grass and wet dirt; and though I was cold and a cripple, I was, for the moment, able to breathe; and I felt at peace, and closed my eyes. I could've slept, I think. Before long, it was true, Jane would arrive at the Pancake House to pick me up and carry me home in our little green car. And what joy it would be, then, to wiggle free from Bernhardt's clutches, and to crawl over to her and embrace her legs, then heave myself up and let her help me to the parking lot. She could prop me against the fender while she opened the car's door, before assisting me into the passenger seat; then—there are a few things I can still accomplish for myself—I might buckle my seat belt, rest my head against the headrest, and shut my tired eyes once again. Beginning at the beginning, leaving nothing to the unscientific imagination, I will tell Jane all about our wonderful psychoanalytic evening. It will take the entire ride home, the full length of Eureka Drive from south to north, from covered bridge to College Hill and across to Granite Farm Road—it will likely take the whole trip to get everything in. Jane is demanding in relation to details. We'll motor up the steep hill that winds past the book factory, and I might lower the passenger window a crack before telling my wife that when Richard hoisted me in his arms, all I could think about was her. This would be my cue to place my hand on Jane's knee, lightly so as to avoid pressing hard and causing her foot to squash down the accelerator; and, squeezing—but not tickling!—her leg, I'd describe my own and the others' after-dinner ascensions, Rebecca's and Sherwin's and Leslie's flights so characteristically undertaken, so perfectly demonstrative of essential qualities in each person's sexual style. Of course I would take care not to neglect a thorough rundown, for Jane's entertainment, of love affairs getting started on the ground and in midair. Would she guess that I might be dropping hints about her trysts with Manuel? How many couples, making their way home and to bed in one another's arms, would, looking back, date their unions to the evening Tom dropped the cinnamon-raisin toast and, raped by Bernhardt, lost the use of his legs, then blasted through the roof? (Speaking of roofs, I'd want to remember to comment on the floating hospital, the golden intensive care unit and, down the hall and around the corner from the ICU, the new, state-of-the-art maternity ward.) I'd even tell Jane about my sojourn with Rebecca at Battlefield Grove—or maybe not?—sitting in our cozy green car as we creep along from red light to red light through the historic downtown row-house grid, a stop-and-start mile before Eureka rises to leave the market district and scale College Hill. Somewhere past the intersection with Woodrow Avenue—one of those dangerous, sloping, four-way stops that, when approached from downhill, require applying the emergency brake—I might work up the courage to let Jane know that I'd had a chance, while floating over my Krakower Institute colleagues' heads, to do some hard thinking about children. Locked in Bernhardt's grasp, I had finally come to understand the meaning and utility of our room at the top of the stairs. I will not be telling Jane anything she does not intuitively know when I say that the thing living there, waiting behind a closed door with so many dead moths scattered across the floor, is my own manhood. Our unborn child is the man she married years ago after walking aimlessly through the dark parts of town, rolling her bicycle through the afternoon light and the falling night, on the summer day when that stranger's dog ran barking from a hillside yard to attack us. Later, a scary bartender told us about his own dead son. First we ran away from the dog, then we ran from the man behind the bar. It was dark out. We were young. We went to bed. We kissed, and, kissing, simply fell in love. Everyone needs someone to fuck, but why should I for one minute believe that my body's needs—or Jane's, for that matter—are crucially different in kind or intensity from the desires and longings felt by thousands of men and women in marriage? Perhaps it is appropriate to say at this juncture that one of the distinguishing pleasures—and illusions—of the psychotherapeutic process is the growing appreciation of personality as a mutable and volatile construct. We tend to scrutinize our own characters, or at least our character traits, all the identifiable likes and dislikes and the old, troublesome habits and so forth, as examples of what we like to call individuality; and it seems to me that, as egotistic individuals, we must at various times use one or another of the sacred languages provided by contemporary scholarship—it's a psychoanalytic vernacular in my case—to utter testimony to ourselves and to the people nearest us, affirming our narcissistic independence from the mass of anonymous folk stumbling without awareness through the world. In this way, asserting and defining separateness, we eventually embrace fear and become—if this makes sense—*uniquely ordinary members of the neighborhood,* living life as intellectual animals who are not afraid to be afraid of sex and sex's outcome, children. I realize that nothing I am saying will strike the average educated thinker as anything more than a self-conscious rehashing of the most basic and thoroughly integrated social ideas, "typically" post-Freudian and, specifically, Adlerian. However, it is important, I think, to consider both pride and humility in relation to events that night at the Pancake House & Bar. Remember that it was April, the season of Easter, the closing of winter. Who was Bernhardt if not my father lifting me in the air? Didn't he smell horribly of aftershave? Hadn't he destroyed, quite possibly indefinitely, my power to walk or even stand upright? Weren't my hands immobilized, my ribs crushed by the man's arms? And what was the meaning of the little dog peering out from Rebecca's neck beneath her hair? In the well-known painting, the dog stares endlessly into a forest world—but this can only be *our* world, I would guess, the concrete, earthly habitation of any viewer—that has been unrecoverably lost to Brueghel's exhausted travelers. Ahead, for the pilgrims, lie open fields and a village with its church's steeple pointing toward heaven. My village that night was the Pancake House; my forest, Battlefield Grove; my steeple, the detached crown of the hospital making its steady way through space toward its rendezvous with the breakfast restaurant. And so it was appropriate—if you stop and think about it—that I would find myself, that night, occupying two or three places simultaneously. I'm not even sure what tense structures to use to describe this order of fragmentation. I was (and had been) in the air over Maria and Manuel, Peter and Dan, and the others from the Institute; I was (and am) curled up on the mound with my head buried in Rebecca's lap. I was in Bernhardt's hug. Hovering overhead inside the Pancake House & Bar, my feet dangling, I had become nothing more, really, than what Richard himself had claimed I was, back at the start of our evening together, when I clambered over his shoulders, then attempted to throw that bread and was, instead, carried aloft in shame. I was this man's tiny baby. With my hand in Rebecca's, and with my father's cock beside me, I was being born. Was it surprising that I might take flight to the battlefield? Was it surprising that I might crave a girl's lap to rest my head on? The grass under blue cloth beneath our bodies smelled like damp hay, and the breeze felt cold. Rain poured down; mist was silver and white; humidity felt heavy against the skin. Here were precisely the atmospheric and barometric conditions under which I might get a reliable boner. I would feel proud to tell Jane everything that had come to pass in the Pancake House, because, you see, I would at last be ready, though without legs and still at heart a child, for sex.

For now, however, I was thinking about black-haired Rebecca and the War for Independence, and about how, in an insignificant battle fought not far from my home in this war, I once stabbed a man, sort of; and about how that man turned out to be a certain girl's father; and about how this girl, this young woman, I should say, came to share intimate family knowledge with me, while, in the mist surrounding us, a legion of presumably friendly, well-intentioned wraiths abandoned their gravesites in order to crouch down in the matted grass and have loud coitus. Shall I risk my professional reputation and insist that this was what I heard? Would I be going, as Maria with her dead tooth likes to point out at every opportunity, too far? I opened my eyes and looked around and saw—not much. Keep in mind that the fog was thick, impressively so. We could not, Rebecca and I, see much of anything beyond each other or our own hands, though we could hear kissing and sighing, ominous noises prevailing in the darkness, gentle thumps and the unsettling echoes of bodies moving and shifting and touching, men and women breathing into one another's mouths at the point before orgasm.

Or was this more likely the wind echoing from hillside to hillside, making low moans in the rain?

"We should get out of here. We're going to get soaked. I'm cold. I don't like it out here. I want to go back to the restaurant. I want to go home!" Rebecca cried out to me.

Home? Was this my Young Woman of Strength?

"I don't like it out here. Why are you talking to me about dead people? You're scaring me. You want to frighten me so I'll sleep with you! But I won't sleep with you! I'm saving myself for Johnny! Johnny loves me. We're going to have a family together, a family of boys who will grow up to be men, and I'm going to be a doctor like Johnny's father, a real doctor with a medical degree and a stethoscope! Take me back. *Please.*"

"Okay."

"What time is it anyway? How long have we been out here? *Tom?* I'm going to get fired."

"You won't be fired," I promised, and felt somewhat sad on her account, glad on the other hand that I was nominally an adult and not a teenager in a crummy job; and I told her, "It's not late."

But it was. The wee hours approached. It was, it must've been, near the time for our inaugural pancake gathering on the south side of town to wind down and, well, end.

What exactly was the hour? Was it after midnight? Before? How much before? How late after?

Leaving the sacred battlefield mound was, luckily, a straightforward proposition. All it required was a little will-power. How nice it might be if everything in life could be accomplished by wishing. How sweet, too, if wishing achieved its own ends.

"Are you sure you don't want to stay here and lie down and, hmm, maybe fool around for a minute?" I asked her. And why not make this passing inquiry? There's nothing wrong, most of the time, with trying. I should say that I did not expect an answer. I was, after all, a man wearing a ring. What would Rebecca see in this husband in his middle years, neither young nor old, and yet, as I imagined it, decrepit in her eyes, so bald and so out of shape, this cripple hobbled by back pain?

"Let's go," I commanded her, and, hand in hand, in tandem, we rose from the ground into the gray mist, aiming our heads to the right, banking northward. "Did you remember to bring the thermos?" I asked Rebecca as we glided high enough to locate—as we had on our trip out—through the fleeting openings in clouds, the shining river where, long ago, the young lieutenant drowned.

"Got it."

But enough about medium-altitude astral projection and the faintly ludicrous picnic appurtenances. Suffice it to say that Rebecca and I found ourselves returned to the Pancake House—where, under the radiant lights hanging from the grimy, tiled ceiling, the situation was no longer what it had been a short time earlier. Not at all.

Dan Graham had disappeared from his place by the aquarium. I could not, looking down from my high perch beneath an omelette pan, find him among the people below. Plenty of smoke filled the room near the ceiling, suggesting that Dan had not been gone long. Perhaps he was in the men's room. Wherever Dan was, it was a relief to know that the fish were, for the time being, safe from capsizing.

Behind the candy counter, off to the far side of the aquarium and partly hidden from view, young Bob and young Katharine were in a clinch. I could not see below the trainees' waists, but I could tell that Bob had weaseled—or should I say "lemured"?—his hands into Katharine's blouse; and, judging from the fabric bunched up as if yanked out of place by hooks between the girl's shoulder blades, I'd say he had her bra undone.

Mike and Elizabeth had made progress in their budding relationship. This pair, each married to a spouse working safely outside the local psychological community, nevertheless knew better than to create a fuss or cause comment at the

Institute offices. A quick glance showed their subtle courtship under way. Mike, not a terrifically sexy man by anyone's standards, was doing his best with what he had, posing casually in a fashion that exhibited his well-developed quadriceps—Mike was a runner, and this was his knee-forward, slightly turned-out "hero" pose from classical theater and art. Elizabeth, in response, reached around with one hand to pull her hair back from her forehead. Her ears popped out in relief.

Someone dropped money in a jukebox. A few people—among these were Terry Kropp and a truly lovely woman I had not before noticed—moved to the room's center, directly underneath Sherwin and Leslie. Who was this woman accompanying Terry? His wife? She was for some reason interested in encouraging Peter Konwicki to get up and dance; to this end she did the thing that a beautiful yet insecure woman will sometimes do if she's drunk enough and the dance floor is uncrowded and she wants the support of a group, shuffling and wiggling a trail from one man to the other and back again, practicing democracy with her beauty. When she held out her hand to summon Peter, he blushed horribly—his whole head went red—and he waved his hands, palms facing out, as if the prospect of doing the bump with this woman and a fellow analyst, even a recent hire like Terry, was nothing less than mortifying. I felt a surprising rush of sympathy and compassion for Peter Konwicki. Why, all of a sudden, did I feel empathy for this man who wants to abolish my after-school programs? I found myself wishing that he would stand up and dance with Terry's wife or girlfriend, whoever she was. Peter seemed, rocking back and forth in his tipped-back chair, lonely and a little withdrawn; and I have to confess that, for reasons I could not name, I liked the man, and wanted him to be happy. Isn't that strange? The music was a pop song I had heard innumerable times on the radio while driving home or to work, several years before; and hearing it now caused me to think about a certain dinner at about that time, during which Jane ordered shellfish that made us both horrendously sick.

Oddly, no waitresses were in sight. Some tables and booths had been cleared, others were in shambles: isolated, unsightly messes of piled plates, cups, and bowls, water glasses stacked into precariously leaning towers on coffee-stained tables. However, no pattern relating the cleared to the neglected tables was apparent. Nor was there any light spilling beneath or between the tall swinging doors leading to and from the kitchen. The kitchen was mysteriously dark. Was the cook on break? The Pancake House & Bar stays open all night, so there must've been an explanation for the missing employees. Possibly the staff were out back smoking. I just don't know.

That teenage boy and his girlfriend were, as I had earlier dreaded, up to no good. I'd figured the kid for a delinquent in the most humdrum, suburban mode, an habitual dope smoker or serious truant. I had not imagined him to be a thief. But that's what he was. In the absence of waitresses, etc., this kid was looting the bar, passing beer bottles from the cooler to the girlfriend as fast as she could hide the bottles under her oversized alpine coat. Cold air steamed from the open refrigerator. The kid reached in with both hands and grabbed bottles by their necks. Actually, as stealing goes, I don't suppose this was a worrisome example. Many adolescents pull exactly these kinds of stunts, then grow up to become responsible and happy. This I know from my practice.

All told, the scene at ground level was what you might expect—an ordinary party broken into factions, staggering through the final stages before collapse. Manuel and Maria sat in their booth looking stunned, as if they could not find the energy to stand and put on coats. I suspect that Maria was waiting to leave with Bernhardt—or, cautiously, a minute before Bernhardt—so that he could get in his purple station wagon and follow her yellow sports car to town. Maria and Manuel watched the dancers, and now and then turned their heads to check out, discreetly, the child-psychology students making out behind the candy counter. Then they peered up at Sherwin and Leslie in the air above the people dancing.

It was this pair, the alcoholic doctor and the orphaned Englishwoman, who presented the evening's most distressing—or most moving?—picture. I feel some reluctance to disclose in detail what I witnessed, purely on grounds that I might prefer to respect the privacy and confidentiality of my friend and his new mistress. On the other hand, this was a pancake restaurant. What the hell, they were fucking. I had to hand it to Leslie. She'd hoisted herself all the way up Sherwin's legs. Hers were wrapped around his back. That's not exactly right: one bare leg was coiled around Sherwin, it's true, and the other, gripped behind the knee by Sherwin with his free hand, the hand not held by Rebecca, extended up and over Lang's shoulder. Leslie's shoe, with its startlingly long and narrow heel pointed toward the ceiling, now and again rubbed against Sherwin's head. Let me say that I could not, observing from above, see any actual, verifiable genital conjunction. But I could see Leslie's skirt hiked up, and Lang's belt unbuckled, his trousers unbuttoned and unzipped. I would have wagered that Sherwin was too drunk to screw, and I would've been wrong. The two were pressed together, making digging motions with their hips.

This as much as anything explained, I decided, the air of relative normalcy, the listless dancing and the sitting quietly in booths and so forth, affected by practically everyone below, my former lover and the others acting like nothing out of the ordinary was going on.

Only Bob and Katharine, the exceptions, were young enough—and mature enough, evidently—to take Sherwin and Leslie's fucking publicly and acrobatically at a height of, I would estimate, ten or more feet off the ground; only these two were the right age to take Sherwin and Leslie as permission to shed inhibitions and act on their own urges.

"Oh my God. Are they doing what I think they're doing?" Rebecca whispered in my ear. She said, "Should a doctor be doing that? I can't believe I'm holding his hand!"

"Don't stare," I said to her.

"I'm not staring," she said.

"It's not polite," I told her.

She said, "What's he doing with her leg? Is that his stomach? I think I'm going to be sick again."

Then Bernhardt spoke. "They've been at it a while. It's hard not to watch a thing like that."

"Try looking away," I suggested.

But of course Richard was right. How often are we given the chance to study people we know in the act of making love?

It was with something like reverence, with a kind of sincere, hushed admiration, that Bernhardt and Rebecca and I watched Sherwin with Leslie in their embrace. Leslie wrapped her arms around Lang, clasping hands behind his neck. Sherwin held Leslie's leg and gently adjusted her, and Rebecca squeezed my hand. I was sure she was squeezing Sherwin's as well; and I noticed that Rebecca's breathing, and Richard's, and mine, had become synchronized with one another's and the lovers' own inhalations and their harmonized movements; we were, Richard and I and Rebecca, unable to stop ourselves from responding to, from obeying—in the ways we touched and brushed against one another, softly—the slow, graceful, controlled periodicity of Sherwin's hips' backward and forward motions against Leslie, moving so nicely opposite him with her eyes closed and her skirt rolled up. Sherwin pushed into Leslie and Bernhardt pushed against me, and, pushing and hugging, clutching and rubbing, he shoved me right up against Rebecca. Rebecca turned, much as Leslie had pivoted her body to accommodate Sherwin's, allowing—I'm referring to Rebecca, not Leslie—her leg to intrude between my legs.

There was no question in my mind that Bernhardt was coming. How can I describe this feeling, except as a kind of incessant, scary, wet, plunging battery against my back? The power of this man to hold me, to use me, was fantastic. His body ground against mine. I could feel and hear his fast breathing against my ear. I could smell him. He jerked and I shook. He shook. A sigh came from him. Little by little, his movement against me slowed. Against my back, and through my shirt, warmth and wetness spread itself out. There was so much. I couldn't see it, but I could feel it. The feeling against my skin was odd, shocking and soothing at the same time. Everything was wet. It had been building up in Bernhardt all night, and now it was over. It was finished. Even the man's panama hat, its brim brushing my neck, could not bother me now. Far below us the dancers twirled, looking over their shoulders from time to time to ascertain the situation near the ceiling, before readdressing themselves to partners and the jukebox music's rhythms.

Light came dully through the restaurant's picture windows. It seemed impossible that it could be morning. Would the waitresses come back? Would the cook? I could make out, through fog and the drizzling rain outside, the pale colors on cars in the parking lot, and the gray trunks of the trees encircling the lot. Then the light outside grew stronger, illuminating the rainwater that streamed down the windows, streaking the panes.

Here at long last came the hospital, casting its light over everything. I could see it—I could see its *light*—outside the window near the booth where Maria and Manuel sat with water and their dregs of cold, black coffee. The huge pyramid coming closer in the sky.

Here it came.

Rebecca forced her leg between my legs. She was communicating to me, with her leg wedged between mine, and

(172)

through the pressure applied by her hand, her fingers working deep into the joints between my knuckles; she was communicating the effect, on her mind and her body, of watching sex happen. She squeezed my hand so hard it hurt. I gripped Rebecca's hand, then released it a tiny bit only, to give her the idea that we could do more than hurt each other; we could rub our hands together and feel, through our fingertips and our palms, a version of intercourse, our chaste rendition of what was taking place beneath us in the air; we could, in other words, fuck with our hands.

Sherwin was going hard with Leslie. Manuel and Maria slouched down in their seats. It was obvious that these two had had a love affair in the past, and that their affair, like mine with Maria, was long finished in some manner that prevented its resurrection under any circumstances. They were my friends, and they were friends to one another, and now they were tired. That was why they sat there doing nothing.

All this time, Bernhardt was holding me, not merely physically, but, more to the point—and in the deep sense made famous by the British Object Relations theorists—emotionally. And yet it was difficult to stay relaxed, everything considered.

Sherwin's hips moved at a pace too rapid for me or Rebecca or Bernhardt to follow or imitate in our breathing; there was nothing for us to do but hang in one another's arms and sweat beneath the skillets. Sherwin, between drunken thrusts, managed to say, "Excellent"—deep, long thrust—"party"—once again moving into Leslie—"Thomas."

It was at this point that a strange and unaccountable thing

happened. A car drove up and stopped outside the Pancake House. I could not see it, because it parked directly out front behind a small, decorative wall. However, I could hear tires crunching the gravel, and I could make out a rattling sound, the motor dying. I could hear, quite clearly, the car door opening, maybe the driver's-side door, maybe the passenger's; and, following this, the expectable metal-and-rubber thud, the door closing. I know by heart these noises made by my own car's out-of-tune engine, its doors unlatching before slamming not so solidly shut; and I thought that this might be—*at last!*—our little green sedan driven by Jane to pick me up.

But it was a man, and not my wife, who walked into the restaurant and stood in the doorway looking around the place.

He was dressed in a dark woolen jacket over a white shirt and black or, perhaps, gray or navy trousers. He wore wire-rimmed glasses and had a smallish nose and a beard trimmed short, and he was, as were so many men gathered that night, nearly bald. What hair he had left was clipped on the top and sides, barbered to match the beard. He was noticeably tall and his ears stood out almost as prominently as Elizabeth Cole's. The man was, by his looks, neither a long-distance traveler nor an insomniac; he appeared, at any rate in my impromptu fantasy about him, as if he had been somewhere in the country for an important dinner that had gone late. He took one look at the scene inside the Pancake House, then turned and walked out.

Here's the strange thing. The man looked like me. He didn't look exactly like me, but he looked something like me—like a happier, better-dressed and better-groomed, entirely better-looking and better-fed, more handsome and successful adaptation of me. That is why I recall him, and why I remember the feelings of shame that came over me when I saw that this was not Jane coming in the door to fetch me home; rather it was a man in a well-cut coat who sauntered in and, I suppose, *took in,* at a glance, as it were, everything required for him to comprehend the situation—the boy and his girlfriend stealing the beer, and Mike and Elizabeth staring into one another's eyes, and the pathetic dancing at the middle of the room. He saw Leslie fucking Sherwin while the rest of us pretended to look away. He saw me being raped.

What must he have thought? He left the restaurant. He'd seen as much as he needed or wanted to see. What future use might he make of it? Light flooded the doorway as he held the door open. He went through into the light. The door closed behind the man, and a moment later the car door opened and closed, and the ignition started the motor, and the car drove away. Possibly someone was with the man in the car. Possibly kids were sleeping in the backseat. Who knows? The car drove away, but the light outside did not diminish. It came in the windows of the Pancake House & Bar. The light was not sunlight, nor was it the light shining from the man's car's headlamps. The light came in the windows, the curtained and uncurtained windows, from east and west and south and north.

Staring into the light, into that glow, I knew—or felt I knew, which in retrospect may be the same or as good; and who can with certainty know what anyone's future will bring?—that my legs were truly dead, and that I would probably never have a son with Jane, and that my own father had, with my complicity, taken my life from me.

My clothes were soaked with sweat and Bernhardt's semen. I felt ashamed, and I was shivering. Was I crying? I think I was. Yes. Bernhardt rocked me in his arms.

"Easy does it," he said to me.

"I don't feel well," I said to him.

"You're going to be all right, Lieutenant," he said to me.

"Something's not right with me," I said to him.

"You're a good man," he said to me.

"Everything hurts," I said to him.

"I've got you, Tom," he said to me.

"I can't move," I said to him.

"Don't try to move," he said to me.

"I want to see Jane," I said, sniffling.

"Jane loves you," he said to me.

"I need to go to the hospital," I said.

"Sshhh."

"Will you take me to the hospital?" I begged my father.

"I will."

"Do you promise?" I asked.

"I promise."

And with that he lifted me up and tossed me in the air, he threw me into the air and, throwing me, let me go. His arms released me, and I released Rebecca's hand, and I was free.

"Goodbye, Tom," said the girl with the dog on her neck, as I flew above the aquarium and the tables and chairs.

"Goodbye, Rebecca," I said to this girl whose father I had probably—no, certainly—stabbed.

"So long, Tom," said Bernhardt, his load lightened, his arms empty of their night's burden.

"Goodbye," I called to him.

"We'll be seeing you later, Tom!" called another voice. This sounded an awful lot like Peter Konwicki—the old adversary transformed, after a night out, into my pal. Or was it Sherwin making a hoarse, fatigued, postcoital adieu? These were my friends saying sad farewells at the end of our supper.

"Feel better!" they all called to me from below.

"Goodbye," I cried back at them. "Goodbye."

I was sorry that Dan was not out of the men's room. What was the problem? Had he accidentally locked himself in? I would have liked to say goodbye to Dan.

"Goodbye," waved Bernhardt and Maria and Manuel. They'd been my booth mates.

"Goodbye!"

"So long!"

"Farewell."

"A bientôt!"

"Goodbye," one last time. "Goodbye."

And this time, when I passed through the roof, I really and truly passed through the roof. It was easy. It happened just like that. I did not, as I knew I would not, feel a thing.

The air was freezing cold outside. Light from above spilled everywhere. We were going to have a frost for sure. What had happened to spring? What would become of Jane's tulips blooming beside our driveway?

I could see the Pancake House roof with its neon sign rigged over the entryway. I heard the thunder from over the river. I saw the parking lot with its towering trees surrounding everyone's cars, the poplars throwing long shadows across the neighboring fields, all the trees and the bushes beneath the trees like a lit-up and windblown train-set forest seen from on high; and I could see, off in the distance, the broken airport.

What about that light cascading down to make the stormy night into day? Need I say that it came from the hospital? It came from the hospital. The hospital had come for me. It was my beacon and my home. It shielded me from the rain. It waited above me.

Before I got inside the hospital, I looked toward the north. I searched this direction and that across the nighttime horizon, to see if I might chance to make out, through the light and the mist and, beyond the awful light, against the outer darkness, any cars on Eureka. And, you know, I did locate, through one brief, tiny opening in the clouds, a small automobile creeping up the steep hill that rises to a flat peak before plummeting like a roller-coaster ride past the book factory, into the covered bridge.

It was good to know that Jane was taking her time, driving safely in the foul weather. I always remind her to buckle her seat belt. To be honest, I sometimes yell at her about this. I'd have to leave it to Manuel or somebody else on earth to tell her, after she arrives at the Pancake House & Bar, where to find me.

In the meantime, and until I felt, for want of a better way of putting it, like a man—until such time, up I went, up, up, into the ICU, with its shiny new beds draped in spotless white sheets. And it occurred to me to wonder whether, had I been able, in my panicked flight from Bernhardt's arms and my own body—had I been able to travel, as I had wanted to travel into the unknown, infinite universe, out past the moon to the farthest stars and beyond—well, I asked myself, then, if the things I might have seen and felt there, out at the edges of space and time—would these things, whatever they might have been (whatever they might *be*), the things that I might have seen (that I might *see*)—might they, I wondered, possibly look or feel to me anything like this ascension into light?

And would Jane, finding me naked on a metal bed on a cold ward, would she crawl into the bed and hold me for a minute, and stroke my head, and whisper sweetly in my ear, over and over again, telling me that, after all, we are married, and she doesn't mind?

ALSO BY DONALD ANTRIM

"Mischievously imagined. . . . Antrim is a wonderful, truly original comic writer." —San Francisco Chronicle

ELECT MR. ROBINSON FOR A BETTER WORLD

In Pete Robinson's seaside suburban town, things have, well, fallen into disrepair. The voters have de-funded schools, the mayor has been drawn and quartered by an angry mob of townsmen, and Turtle Pond Park is stocked with claymore mines. Pete Robinson, a third grade teacher who keeps a 1:32 scale model of an Inquisition dungeon in his basement, wants to open a new school. In his effort to do so he stumbles upon another idea: he should run for mayor. Uniquely hilarious, Antrim's first novel is a disturbingly insightful tale of a world frighteningly similar to the one in which we live.

Fiction/Literature/0-375-72503-2

THE HUNDRED BROTHERS

There's Rob, Bob, Tom, Paul, Ralph, and Phil; Siegfried, the sculptor in burning steel; blind Albert and ninety-three-year-old Hiram; Foster, the New Age psychoanalyst; and Maxwell, the botanist, who, since returning from the rain forest, has seemed a bit screwed up. When Antrim brings them together with their eighty-nine equally eccentric kinsmen in the decaying library of their family estate for cocktails, a light supper, and a little ritual sacrifice, the result suggests a high-speed collision between *The Brothers Karamazov* and the Brothers Marx. Moving swiftly from slapstick to horror and back, *The Hundred Brothers* provides insights into the agonies of kinship that are as serious as they are hilarious.

Fiction/Literature/0-679-76942-0